Cotton Nails

Cotton Nails © 2022 Cameron Beatty.
All Rights Reserved.

No part of this book may be reproduced in any form or by any electronic or mechanical means including information storage and retrieval systems, without permission in writing from the author. The only exception is by a reviewer, who may quote short excerpts in a review.

This book is a work of fiction. Names, characters, places, and incidents either are products of the author's imagination or are used fictitiously. Any resemblance to actual persons, living or dead, events, or locales is entirely coincidental.

Printed in Australia

First Printing: April 2022

Shawline Publishing Group Pty Ltd
www.shawlinepublishing.com.au

Paperback ISBN- 9781922701473

Ebook ISBN- 9781922701534

A catalogue record for this book is available from the National Library of Australia

Cotton Nails

CAMERON BEATTY

I'd like to thank my dog for being a sentient being that never lets me down.

Prologue

I had a feeling tonight would end this way. I'm not sure why. Sometimes nothing happens on our shifts - we chase false alarms or don't get many call-outs. But at other times, there's enough blood and guts to spill into your nightmares. You just never know.

I'm tired, though, and I've noticed this more and more lately. I'm tired of feeling this way, and I'm tired of these mean-spirited reminders that have given my eyes a certain look about them.

I keep playing along with CPR, but the silence is growing, and we need to get the cops here quick.

Elvis has frozen up, so Bailes says to him, maybe we should call off the ambos; we've got this under control.

"There's no need to bring them here into this."

He's trying to prompt him to get upstairs where there's radio reception to call in the cops, but when the guy in the doorway says, "Bring them into what?" I know it's all about to kick off.

That's when I cease compressions and stand up. I see the outline of the man in the doorway.

He says, "I think it's best if we all stay put for the moment."

"Why?" I take a step towards him. Elvis and Bailes step up behind me too.

I'm tired of this. We've been brought here tonight, and it might be meaningless to everyone, but it means something to me. It doesn't feel like a coincidence. I start to lose the feeling in my hands, and I have to breathe.

My mind races. I go to all sorts of places. I've lost touch with a lot of things in my life. There's a meanness in me now that I have to live with, and it's uncomfortable. I'm not what they say I am, but I am a little bit, and maybe it's enough to see me through tonight.

Odey is fighting back the tears. He tries to reason with the guy, but it's useless. I can't see if he's armed, but I assume he is. I guess I'm waiting for something, a definite sign. I want to be sure because I know what could happen.

Then we hear the footsteps closing in. They're coming down the stairs towards us. I'm looking at the shadow of the man in the doorway, and he's looking right back at us. He's about four metres away, but there are four of us and only one of him for the moment.

The footsteps are getting closer. This moment stretches out for a long time, but the instant the flickering light finally dies completely, he yells, "In here, now," and we all rush him.

It's over pretty quickly, and later on, I find myself back on the surface, sitting on the bonnet of a police car with Odey, red and blue lights flashing over us. There's blood on my face and hands, Odey can't put weight on his legs, and I'm not sure about Elvis or Bailes.

There's a crowd of onlookers around us just outside the lights. They're quiet, though, and I keep my eyes down because I don't want to talk to the police just yet.

That's when Odey says to me, "Jesus Christ, Riley, I really want to go home."

My name is Riley. I'm the one standing there in the middle with his shirt un-tucked.

1.

"Are you watching closely?"

This is the first thing I hear when I walk into the mess, a line that, for some reason, jolts me awake as I push open the door. I leave my hands sort of outstretched for a couple of seconds before I drop them down to my sides with a slight thud.

"Hey Riley," I hear somewhere to my left, "how's the training going?"

I say it's going OK.

"Cool. Make sure you let me know when you're fighting next. I'll bring the guys from 62. They'll love it."

"Will do."

I keep moving past the table where the guys from the previous shift talk about the car fire they were called out to last night; awoke them just after midnight, they say.

"Turned out it was actually on fire. We had to put water on it and everything. Crazy."

I make my way towards the kitchen area. Bailes, Odey, and CJ are sitting up on the bench. Coop leans against the wall with his arms crossed, grinning at me.

"Lads," I say.

"Hey Riley, we were just talking about you," Coop says.

"Oh yeah?" I begin to fix myself a coffee at the machine.

"Yeah. You remember that house fire we went to last year?"

I busy myself at the machine with my back to them. He tells them about how he was operating the pump to give me water on the hose reel, that he was really distracted because he couldn't find a hydrant. Then all of a sudden, I appeared out through the front door with that unconscious woman in my arms.

"Holy shit, Coop," Odey says, "I didn't know you were there."

"Yeah, it was Riley and me that day. We got a proper save and everything."

"That is so cool," Odey says.

"It wasn't like that," is all I say, and I wait for the conversation to move on. Odey then groans about wishing something like that would happen to him, so I finish up with my coffee and turn back around.

"I've had nothing, but false alarms and friggin' cat saves since I got in."

"Someone's got to save the cats, Odey." CJ slaps him on the shoulder. "And look at it this way, when you're saving cats, you get recognition for it. You get to come down the ladder and hand it over to the distraught lady who is forever indebted to you."

Lefty's trying to edge his way into the conversation. He crosses his arms and takes up a position next to CJ on the bench. He grins awkwardly and nods.

"When you're at a house fire, no one even really gets to see you in action. It's like it may as well not have happened."

Odey sighs. "I guess you're right."

Coop winks at him. "Don't worry, champ. You'll get a fire soon."

Lefty clears his throat like he's going to say something but then reconsiders – there is a moment where everyone looks at him, which quickly passes – before Bunker's dry voice comes over the PA.

"A Shift, muster time. Everyone report to the engine bay."

He then sighs quite deliberately into the mic before clicking off.

"It's that time, lads," Bailes says, swivelling himself from the bench. "Time to look sharp."

As if part of a collective life force, everyone slowly moves towards the change room doors in a giant gaggle. Spoon appears to my left, grinning.

"Hey Riley," he says, "how's the training going?" He throws a few playful punches at me, which I return.

I tell him it's going OK.

"Cool, man."

We push through the doors, walking past Brian and Barry from B Shift as they get changed into their civilian clothes.

"I told you," Brian says, "keep your shit on your side of the bench."

"It's not on your side, Barry."

"Well, what do you call that, Brian?"

"You're seeing things, man. You need help."

There is some more bickering from the two, which fades inconsequentially into the background as the group makes its way through the toilets towards the stairwell. Spoon decides he's not taking the stairs today and runs past me, throwing himself at the fire pole. He turns around and fires me a grin before he disappears down the well.

"Hey, Riley."

I turn my head. It's Stacks. His face is held in its usual deadpan expression, and his feet scuff a little as he drags his lumbering frame behind me.

"Hey, Stacks."

I ask him how he is.

"The same old, I guess." He shrugs and sighs. "It never really changes, does it? Just when you think you've had some kind of grand life revelation, you realise it's just another temporary moment of premature enlightenment."

He stops in his tracks and touches his pocket.

"Shit," he says, "I've lost my keys."

The door to the stairway then closes behind me, separating us, and for a moment, Stacks catches my eye through the window (a blank, empty look) before I turn and move on down the stairs.

The stairwell is covered in messages from years ago.

"Watch your step, Torpes."

"False alarms will be the death of us."

… As well as the Fire Fighters Union motto, written in big, bold, red lettering on the wall at the corner: "Stand fast, stand together."

I follow on in the middle of the crowd. As I reach the bottom of the stairs somewhere behind me, I hear Coop yell out, "That's not what your mum said last night, Frenchy!"

I keep moving past the PPE cages holding everyone's helmets and turnout boots, and protective clothing before I push through the engine bay doors. The space then opens up in front of me: the fire trucks sitting in a row to my left, the watch room, where Bunker sits behind the window with his feet up on the desk, at the opposite end of the engine bay, and to my right the remnants of a basketball hoop that was destroyed last month when Bailes attempted a slam dunk ("Fuck man," he said, "I almost had it. Those bolts were cheaply made anyway.").

We move towards the edge of the engine bay, where we

loosely congregate into a line. Everyone keeps filing out of the door one after the other. Magoo, Frenchy, Coop, who does a little jump and hits the top of the door frame on his way through; CJ is standing to my left, Odey to my right, and as I look up, I see Drillbit making his way past me, one eyebrow raised. At the last moment, I raise my hand by my waist, which he casually high fives. He then takes another few steps and spins on the spot into the line, somewhere to my right.

There's a dull murmur, laughter mixed in with individual conversations. I can hear a voice – Tonto, I think – talking about the football game on the weekend. Odey is talking about a party he went to on his days off, and Lefty is laughing and saying "Yeah," a lot.

A man appears in the doorway. I recognise him from the previous shift, although I don't know his name. For some reason, he looks at me, of all people, and asks if everyone's in today, and if not does he need to hang around to fill the shortage.

I tell him I have no idea, that I wish I could answer his question, but I just don't know. He looks back at me, frowns as if uncertain what to say next, and then just recedes back through the doorway, disappearing from sight, an unnecessarily dramatic image for something so insignificant.

Before long, one of our officers, Mumbles, appears with a clipboard in hand. Next to me, Odey snaps himself to attention in mock formality.

"How-is-everyone?"

Mumbles says it quickly as if it were one word. No one responds, but he says "Good" anyway and then begins to read the gear sheet for the week, allocating everyone a position on a truck. Driving Pumper A is Bailes, and on the back is Odey and myself, while Coop is driving Pumper B with CJ on the back to tell him where to go when he forgets where he is.

"You're my eyes and ears out there," Coop says.

"I gotcha, man." CJ pats him on the back.

Driving the Ladder Extension is Spoon, who whoops loudly at this news, with Frenchy in the passenger seat. The Comms Unit this week will be manned by Magoo and Stacks, who still haven't spoken to each other since Magoo told everyone, "as a joke," that Stacks was born with only one testicle.

On the Ultra Large Pumper will be Drillbit and Tonto. Finally, all by himself on the Zone Car will be Lefty, who pretends to be excited by this news with a little fist pump, only no one notices.

"That's-it-then," Mumbles says, eyeing the clipboard, "Fall-out-and-check-the-gear."

He casts his eyes up and down the line, looking for someone until he finds me. Instinctively I recoil a little. Under his breath, he says something completely indecipherable before turning and walking away.

I'm mildly concerned. I don't know what he said or why he said it specifically to me. Does he want me to follow him? Is something required of me today that I'm not aware of? Or what's more likely, am I in trouble for something?

But I don't budge. I just stand there with my hands in my pockets. Within seconds, as everyone breaks out of the line and mills about me in little, segregated groups, I completely forget that this interaction ever took place.

This is where I work. This is my crew, and this is my world four days a week when I'm on shift. The time passes in cycles. Cycles of four days that come and go and blend into one another, overlapping themselves endlessly.

What happens now is that we all check the trucks. First, I grab my gear from my PPE cage, my turnout boots and pants, helmet and tunic, and shoulder my way through the door back into the engine bay, where I ditch my stuff at the door of my truck. Inside the truck, Odey is telling Bailes, who's in the driver's seat, about the girl he almost hooked up with at the party on the weekend.

"I was so close, man," he whines, "I thought I had it in the bag. She was a stunner too, real good-looking."

Bailes takes this in, nodding to himself sternly.

"So, like, what happened?"

"I don't know." Odey groans and throws his hands to his face as he slides down in his seat.

I pull the breathing apparatus from its spot behind my seat and begin conducting its daily check. I turn on the air cylinder, and the unit beeps loudly.

"She was leading me on all night. And I even asked one of her friends if she had a boyfriend."

Bailes leans in a little. "And?"

"And she didn't. So, I'm thinking I'm good to go."

There's a knock at my door. I look down to see Coop. I wind down the window. "Are you guys all in for lunch?" he asks.

"What's for lunch?" I say.

"I don't know yet. But are you in?"

"I'm in," Bailes cries out.

"Me too," Odey yells over my shoulder.

"That's two," Coop says. He then brings his gaze to me. "What about you?" There's a tension behind his eyes – it's slight, but I can definitely see it – and when I falter momentarily, he decides to add, "Everyone's doing it, Riley."

"Well," I say, "I better go in for lunch then."

"Good," Coop says, "good," and walks away.

"So anyway," Odey pushes on, "it gets to the end of the night, and I'm thinking I need to at the very least get her number."

"Right," Bailes frowns.

At this point, my breathing apparatus has begun beeping

at me. It's not supposed to do this. I check the screen on the receiver for answers but find none. It keeps beeping, and after a while, I just decide to turn the thing off and replace it back in its holder behind my seat. This is my solution to the problem.

"So, we're chatting away, and I casually ask if I can get her number – no big deal."

"And what did she say?"

Odey pauses and draws in a deep breath. "She just said, 'no.'"

"She just said, 'no'?"

Odey nods. "She just said, 'no.' Without any follow up explanation. Then," he says, "she just turned and walked away." He throws up his arms. "I ask you, what the fuck is that all about?"

"I don't know, Odey," Bailes says. "Riley, what do you think?"

"Hmm." I think it over. "Did you tell her you were a firefighter?"

"It was the first thing I told her!"

"Then I don't know then."

Odey begins groaning, which morphs into a kind of guttural growl, and he slides all the way down to the floor of the truck where he moans, "Why?" over and over, rolling back and forth in agony.

I tell him that these things happen, to not let it defeat him – he's better than that. Life will go on.

"You always know to say the right thing, Riley," Bailes says.

I purse my face up and nod knowingly.

"I was gunning for it, Riley," Odey moans from his back, making a kung fu gesture with his hands. "Gunning straight for it. I had it. It was right there." He holds his hands out in front of him for a while before pursing his lips together in defeat. His arms collapse beside him.

"Hey, are we doing something today?" Bailes looks at me.

"I don't know."

"I thought Mumbles said we were doing something."

"Like what?"

Odey begins collecting himself with some breathing exercises on the ground.

"I thought he said we were doing a drill, or we had a meeting or something."

"It's a union meeting," Odey says from the ground, keeping his eyes closed. "We're having it after lunch in the mess."

"Oh," I pause. "do we have to go?"

"No." Odey opens his eyes and looks at me. "You don't have to."

"But everyone's doing it?"

"Exactly."

"Right." I turn to Bailes in the driver's seat and ask him if he wants me to check over anything else in the truck. He looks around vacantly at the checklists he's managed to scatter around himself.

"Nah, it's probably all under control."

"Cool."

I jump out of the truck and throw the door shut before making my way across the engine bay. Drillbit and CJ are playing cricket with a tennis ball, and as Drillbit belts the ball, he sends it hurtling against the window of the office, adjacent to the watch room. As the officers snap their heads up behind the glass, Drillbit drops the bat and runs away, screaming.

"It was CJ! You all saw it!"

Amongst all the officers up there, the only one who really seems annoyed is The Pinch. He catches my eye for a second, but I quickly look away.

My hands return themselves to my pockets, and I shoulder my way through the door before heading for the stairs. By the

PPE cages, I catch Tonto, our union delegate, telling Magoo, "I can't believe this is happening. Have they not thought about us? It's tradition, dammit. No one bypasses the union!"

"Yeah," Magoo clears his throat. "Definitely."

I make my way up the stairs. I walk through the change rooms. Brian and Barry from B Shift have disappeared, but there's a red line in permanent marker down the middle of the bench between their lockers. There's also some writing on either side of the line: 'Brian's side' and "Barry's side".

I push my way through the door back out into the mess again, where Spoon is cooking something on the stove.

"I'm making omelettes," he says, "for everyone."

He's wearing an apron and has acquired a chef's hat from somewhere, which sits a bit to one side as he slides around the kitchen space, his heels screeching a little against the floor.

I take a seat at the table. I grab the newspaper that's three days old and begin to flick through the pages. In my pocket, my phone buzzes. It's a text from the union. "Urgent." it reads, "Union bulletin that requires your immediate viewing," with a link to a website attached. And then, at the end of the message, the line, "Take care of your heroes."

I close the message and slide my phone back into my pocket. Odey walks in through the door. He stops in front of me and flexes his muscles in silence, checking to see that I'm still up for the gym session we had planned for later. I nod. He nods back and disappears through the other door.

I don't know what to expect from today. Perhaps we will be busy. Or perhaps things will be quiet. Or maybe, by chance, something will happen that I've never seen before. Something that might kickstart an entirely new phase of my life, for better or for worse, an incident that propels me into a world of chaotic revelations and dramatic turnarounds that sees me either recoil in dread or advance peacefully into another chapter.

But for now, I'm just sitting in the mess with my knee pried up against the table's edge, reading yesterday's news. Tonto bursts in through the door with Frenchy and Lefty. They're talking about footy. This team against that team, pros versus cons, individual players' attributes that might shift the tide in either direction and the like. They sit down at the other end of the table.

At the same time, Bunker's voice comes over the PA.

"Due to popular demand, lunch today will be souvlakis. Please place your orders with me in the watch room. I will write them down, and hopefully, by lunchtime, all your wettest dreams will come true."

He lingers on the PA for a second. I hear some shuffling around before he clicks off.

I stare at the newspaper in front of me, but as the conversation at the end of the table pushes on, Tonto and Frenchy passionately debate their views on which of their teams is better. Lefty, who hasn't really said much thus far, turns to me and says, "Riley doesn't follow footy. Do you, Riley?"

Tonto's head snaps around. "Huh?"

"Riley. He doesn't follow footy."

Tonto frowns. "Wait, what do you mean?"

Lefty shrugs and gestures to me. "Ask him."

"Don't you follow footy, Riley?"

I look up over the paper, shake my head, lower my gaze and turn a page.

"Oh, so you're more of a rugby man, is that it?"

My head shakes again.

Tonto looks away for a moment. "Soccer?"

I look back up at him. "No."

A darkness overcomes Tonto. The whole room seems to dim. All background noise fades away, and the image of Tonto sort of grows in front of me. His eyes narrow.

"What exactly are you saying?"

Coop walks into the room. Straight away, he senses the tension and stops dead in his tracks.

"Riley," Tonto makes a troubled face like I've just offered up some kind of diabolical, world-shattering confession. "I don't understand this."

In the background, Coop quickly holds out a hand.

"It's OK, Tonto," he says, "relax your sphincters. Riley's a boxer."

"Oh, you're a boxer." Tonto exhales. "Oh, that's OK then." The shadows of doubt resolve, and the background hum of activity returns. The force regains its balance.

Tonto holds a hand across his chest.

"Phew," he says. "I didn't realise that. Wow. OK."

Lefty goes to say something on the matter, but Tonto cuts him off. "We should push you up the front when we have to deal with crazies at EMR jobs."

"Hells yes," Frenchy says. "Remember that time when the guys from station 54 got called to that drug overdose a while back at that house where all those junkies were squatting?"

Tonto pauses. "Oh yeah. Was that the one where one of the druggies started flicking his blood at our boys, trying to scare us away?"

"Yep. Right before he got himself knocked the fuck out by Riley over here."

"That was you?" Tonto asks me.

I shake my head.

"What are you on about?" Frenchy leans across the table.

I shrug. "That wasn't me. I wasn't even there."

Frenchy blinks a few times. He tells me that it was me, and everyone knows it.

"It was the talk of the brigade for like, six months after it happened. I know there was legal stuff you needed to duck back then to avoid the shit storm that might have been made over it. But that's over now. You don't need to deny it to us."

"It wasn't me. I wasn't even at station 54 when that happened. I was at 61." Everyone's looking at me. "What?"

"I tried my hand at boxing once," I hear to my right. It's Stacks. He's appeared, sitting right next to me. I didn't see or even hear him enter the room.

"Wasn't really my thing. I guess I'm not that good at all that kind of stuff." He shrugs. "I gave it a good go too. I really tried, but I just didn't seem to ever get any better at it."

"Well," Tonto says, "it's not really your kind of sport, Stacks."

"Oh," Stacks groans, "Here we go."

"Yes. A giant girly man like you should stick to a less robust activity. Is cottaging a sport? I can see you doing that. Hanging with the gays and getting your workouts that way."

Frenchy laughs, and the two high-five each other. They then embark on a homophobic cavalcade, which goes on forever.

"Girly man," Stacks repeats, monotone. "Right." He turns to me. "You know I played footy for a long time until I was about twenty-five. I played ruck. I almost made it to the big leagues, but I broke my ankle and had to give it up."

I tell him I didn't know that. I'm in automatic pilot.

"That's weird because I tell people all the time. I've told Tonto like three times, but he either never remembers or just refuses to acknowledge it." He looks at Tonto, who's laughing along with Frenchy as they compare homophobic slurs.

"Tonto," Stacks says, raising his voice. "Tonto!"

But Tonto doesn't even react, just keeps joking with Frenchy – it's like he's moved to another room.

Stacks turns back to me. "See? Nothing."

There's something familiar about this scene here. I feel that I've seen it before, at another station, somewhere. I narrow my eyes a little. It's triggered something.

I turn to Stacks, who is looking at me strangely, but before I can say anything, the tones sound.

The electronic siren blares over the PA system as the computer-generated voiceover tells us the call.

"Pumper 53A," it says, "for a Fire Indicator Panel at 320 Alfred St."

I use my foot to push my chair back from the table and walk towards the door.

"Godspeed, Riley," Stacks says behind me. My left ear starts ringing again.

I throw him a wave with the back of my hand over the shoulder and push through the door, making my way through the locker room. In the hallway on the other side, I can hear Odey and Bailes sprinting their way towards the fire poles.

"Don't panic," Odey screams. "No one panic!"

I pull open the door to the hallway and see Bailes dramatically throw himself onto the fire pole, but then, as he slides down, he moans, "My balls!"

I'm next down, and once I hit the ground, I move past the LCD screen with an enlarged map of the address for the call. I give it a quick glance.

I reach my side of the truck only to discover that Lefty, for some reason, has come downstairs too. He's staring at a printout of the map, frowning very seriously.

"You'll turn right out of the station," he says to me, "then you'll follow Boyd St until it turns into Alfred."

I step into my boots and pull up my overtrousers.

"Then," Lefty pushes on, "you'll keep moving down Alfred–"

But I'm already in the truck, and I close the door on Lefty mid-sentence. We tear out of the engine bay, lights and sirens blaring, leaving him staring after us vacantly with the little piece of paper in his hand and no one to talk about it with.

I ask Bailes if he knows where the call is.

He says that he does.

"Cool," I say.

I don't know which officer we have with us today, and I stare at the back of his head in the front passenger's seat for a moment before he turns around. It's Elvis. He sees me and grins.

"Riley."

"Elvis."

We barrel down the tram tracks as Odey flaps about next to me, pulling on his tunic. He accidentally hits me a few times with the sleeve. In response, I kind of smoosh his face a bit with the palm of my hand, pushing him away.

I slide my arms through the straps of the breathing apparatus fixed into my seat and tighten them against my shoulders, then grab a radio and a torch from the panel in front of me and fix them to the front of my tunic.

"Fire ground 15," Elvis calls out from the front.

"15," I echo as I tune my radio to the right channel.

We reach the corner of Boyd to Alfred, passing through the intersection at high speed. Traffic comes to a halt as we run the red light. A group of girls stop and wave at us, kebab shop sure things. Bailes has told me he knows where he's going, and I take his word for it. I don't open up the street directory or anything.

"Here we are, lads," Bailes says after a while.

COTTON NAILS

We swerve onto the other side of the road by the footpath. Clearly, the evacuation point: a crowd of people from the building, an office complex, are milling about. I push the lever to my side, releasing the breathing apparatus from my seat, and hop out of the truck.

As I throw open one of the side compartments, pulling the axe from its holder, Pumper 54 pulls up across the street, Dreads in the driver's seat. He makes a face at me. I answer with a point of the finger.

Odey grabs the high-rise kit from the compartment. We follow on behind Elvis, pushing our way through to the front door, where a security guard directs us down a hallway to the Fire Indicator Panel. Elvis opens the panel door, and I lean myself against the wall in the background, the axe across one shoulder. Odey tells me he hopes the detector isn't all the way up on the top floor. It would be a long walk.

"Me too, Odey," I say, "me too."

Then Twelve Gauge, the officer from Pumper 54, walks straight past me to Elvis. He talks to him for a moment but then turns around and looks at me. At this point, I realise I've left my helmet in the truck, but it's too late to do anything about this now – I'm committed. There's no turning back.

Twelve Gauge looks at me, I can see, wanting to tell me off for this minor indiscretion. Still, something about the way I'm looking at him (blankly, without really moving much) makes him reconsider.

"Hi Riley," he ends up saying.

"Hi, Twelve Gauge."

He looks away for a second before looking back again.

"It was good having you with us last month."

I smile, and my left ear starts ringing.

Out of the corner of my eye, Odey looks at me dubiously. I raise an eyebrow at him.

"Alright guys," Elvis says, "it's on the fifth floor somewhere, near the rear office." He turns to the security guard. "Can you take us there?"

"Yeah," he says, "but the elevators aren't working. We'll have to take the stairs."

This gets a small groan out of me as we follow behind the security guard, pushing through the masses of people still evacuating the building. Lots of people look at me. I see Odey give a wink to a girl who blushes.

He asks me if I saw that. I tell him that I did.

Eventually, we reach the fifth floor. I've already undone my jacket, and it's probably only a matter of time before my cumbersome breathing apparatus finds itself on the ground somewhere. It doesn't really matter; these calls are always false alarms anyway.

"I'll go this way," I say and spear off down the hallway to my right. Our goal at this stage is to find the activated smoke detector. This can be identified by a single, fixed red light that shines from its base. We have to find the activated detector, so we can confirm that the building is not on fire, so we can reset the alarm in order to come back out at a later date when it activates itself again. You don't really need to be a firefighter to do this part of the job. Most people could probably manage this on their own.

As predicted, my breathing apparatus slides down from my shoulder to the ground in the hallway as I wander along, gazing up idly at the roof. I keep the axe with me, though, and I kind of swing it loosely by my side as I scuff my way along the carpet.

"Seen anything yet, Riley?" Odey's voice comes through the radio.

I push the receiver. "All quiet on the Western Front, mate."

"I'm just checking this corridor back here."

I glance around. "Back where?"

"Here?"

"Where's here?"

"I don't know exactly." He pauses. "Behind you somewhere."

There is a longer pause before I hear Odey making bird calls through the hallways.

"Wah-waaaaaaaaaahr, wah-waaaaaaahr, wah-waaaaaaaahr!"

I respond with my own.

"Cah-coooooorrr, cah-coooooorrr, cah-coooooorr."

A long silence follows. And then Elvis joins in somewhere with a peacock cry.

My phone buzzes in my pocket. I pull it out to find another text from the union.

"You deserve better," it reads, "don't let the Brigade push you around. Make your voice heard at tomorrow's rally. Attendance crucial." I delete the message and replace the phone in my pocket as I continue searching for the detector.

And then I find it, sitting alone in the hallway, surrounded by empty office cubicles. There's no definable reason why it activated. Maybe someone burnt some toast in the kitchenette all the way over there, and a zephyr of smoke found its way into the detector, or maybe someone tried to eliminate a fly with some bug spray, which in turn activated the alarm. Or maybe it just set itself off because it was bored and developed a god complex. Either way, the simple fact remains that this is yet another false alarm.

I hit the receiver on my radio.

"Found it, Elvis. It's," I pause, "over here."

"Where?" he asks.

I make a few more bird noises.

"Gotcha. Be there in a tick."

After a few seconds, Elvis appears around the corner, followed by Odey, who widens his eyes and says, "Nice work Riley. Sterling effort."

Elvis takes up a position beneath the detector and stares at it for a long time, searching it for answers. Eventually, I say, "Elvis, it appears to be a false alarm."

And he looks back at me and says, "Riley, I think you're right."

By the time I make it back downstairs, I have my BA slung over one shoulder with the mask dangling down by my side. I walk past the Fire Indicator Panel where Twelve Gauge is telling off one of the guys from his station, someone I've probably been introduced to several times before but inevitably forgotten. I hear the word "unacceptable" used twice. The guy nods.

"Later," I say as I walk through the door.

But Twelve Gauge doesn't say anything. Out of the corner of my eye, I see him staring at me. My face mask clips the sliding door on my way out.

Back in the truck, I secure my BA and replace the torch and radio to the panel.

"How was it?" Bailes asks.

"About as good as it gets."

"And how was Twelve Gauge? Was it weird bumping into him again?"

I think about it for a second. "No."

Bailes nods. "Yeah. You guys haven't really spoken after that thing last month, have you?"

I stare straight through him.

"Did he start getting into the building staff for," he makes inverted commas with his hands, "'inefficient execution of evacuation procedures'?"

"No. But he was telling off one of his guys about something."

Bailes sighs. "He just can't help himself, can he? He's a special kind of bloke."

He looks around, tapping a pen against the steering wheel.

"Are you going to that union rally tomorrow?"

"No." He goes quiet for a second.

"Tonto might not like that ... I reckon everyone else is going."

Odey appears in the other doorway.

"Get this thing off me," he groans and hurriedly shakes off his BA. "Phew," he says, pulling off his tunic, "I'm as warm as a Turkish brothel, 'yo'."

I hear a beeping horn and turn my head to see Elvis crossing the road, holding out a hand to slow an advancing car. He moves forward but hesitates, and as he does so, it lurches forward a tad. So, begins a kind of baulking, stop/start hand-raising routine before he finally takes his chances and scurries across the street. The driver throws his hand out of the window and guns it up the road.

Elvis opens the front passenger door.

"Je-sus," he says, "some people."

He pulls off his helmet.

"A job well-done, boys. You did me proud out there. Now," he points his hand like a gun at Bailes, "take us home."

I find myself back at the station, walking up the stairs from the engine bay.

"Gym, soon," Odey yells out somewhere behind me.

I tell him, yeah, we'll do it soon.

"Cool, man."

Over the PA comes some awkward clearing of the throat,

followed by Bunker's voice.

"A friendly reminder that after lunch, there will be a union meeting … in the lecture room next to the watch room." He pauses, sighs, then adds, "… down here near me."

There is another pause.

"… Please be prompt in your arrival. Time is of the essence here. And … your punctuality will be appreciated by those who appreciate such things. Thank you."

He clicks off as I shoulder my way through the door to the bedding hallway. I walk up the corridor, passing the bed partitions on my left. I can hear some mumbling up ahead, and a bit further on, I catch a glimpse of Tonto on the phone in one of the bed spaces. He is talking in hushed tones, and I hear him say something about "flushing out the scabs" and "separating the men from the boys."

He sees me walking by and instantly stops talking. I see his head slowly turn in the darkness as I move past, and he doesn't resume talking until I open the door to the TV room.

To my left, CJ is playing darts with Frenchy and Magoo.

"Riley," he says. "How was it?"

I tell him we made history.

"Right on." Behind him, Stacks sits on the pool table with his arms crossed. He gazes at the dart board like it represents something to him, a goal, a totemistic belief of some kind, and visibly sighs.

I redirect myself to the right, where I see a bunch of the guys watching TV. I don't know what they're watching, but Coop points to the screen and exclaims, "Look at those cans. That's what I call a can-do attitude!" As quickly as he can make this observation, a competition for who can jeer the loudest erupts, and the three couches are filled with broken heroes pointing, cheering, rolling around in spontaneous revelry.

I'm through the next door now to the lockers, and before

the door swings shut behind me, I hear someone yell, "Yeah! Fuckin huge. A fucken breasteraunt!" As I make my way to my locker, I catch something out of the corner of my eye. It's Lefty. He's hovering around one of the lockers, but when he sees me, he drops his gaze and quickly scuttles past me with a guilty look. I keep my eyes on him and watch him make his way down the locker rooms until he exits at the door at the end, but not before throwing me a quick glance to see if I'm still looking at him, which I am.

The door closes quietly behind him, leaving me in the silence of the room. I turn my head to the locker that Lefty was standing by. Something's stuck to the door. I move in for a closer look.

It's Stacks' locker, and I see that Lefty has stuck on a photo of a gay man's body at Mardi Gras with Stacks' head photoshopped onto it. I look back to the door where Lefty was only moments ago as if expecting to see him peeking through the window at me but see nothing. He's gone. But I know that from now on, whenever we catch each other's eye, this moment will stay with us. There is a truth to this that will remain with me. Something surges within me. It rises for a moment but then subsides.

I then hear a door open. Someone walks in whistling the theme tune to Hawaii Five-O, and straight away, I know it must be Odey. I move down the corridor and pick up a shoe from one of the benches – probably Coop's, he's always leaving his stuff lying around – before I round the aisle and toss it directly at Odey's feet.

"Jesus!" he screams, throwing himself back into his locker.

"Come on," I turn back around and walk away, "let's go to the gym."

"Why the fuck don't my biceps ever seem to grow?" Odey inspects his arms in the mirror by the free weights.

I tell him it's complicated.

"I don't care if I don't have big legs. I don't even care if I don't have a big chest." He turns to me. "But the biceps – they're like the man equivalent of cleavage on a girl. It's the first thing you notice. It's the first superficial judgment you make about someone." He moves his arms around a bit before performing a flex in the mirror. "And right now," Odey sighs, "I'm on the dude equivalent of an A cup." He then pauses before adding, "At best."

I'm sitting next to Odey on a bench. He looks at the size difference between my dumbbells and his and says, "For fuck's sake Riley."

Odey has his music playing on the speakers. At the moment, we're listening to 'Rescue Me' by Fontella Bass. He's turned the music up as far as it will go (five minutes ago, I heard Magoo scream, "Keep it fucking down in there!" on the other side of the door, "We're trying to play darts in here. It's war, dammit!").

I'm wearing my gym gear, but I have my brigade t-shirt with me in case the tones sound and I have to jump on the truck. I'm hoping they won't. And even if they do sound, I also know that I'll probably just leave my t-shirt where it is and jump on the truck in my gym gear. It's the more likely scenario.

Odey does a little dance to the music. "Hey," he says, "are you going to the union rally tomorrow?"

I tell him that I don't think I'm going to make it.

Odey nods, still looking at himself in the mirror – I don't know if he's listening or not. "It should be good," he says, "the nurses from St Alfred's are coming. Spoon's got a friend who works there, some hot girl I'm trying to get him to set me up with."

Odey wraps his hands around one of the dumbbells on the rack. A look of intense concentration overcomes him as he poises himself. He then sucks in a breath and tries to push the dumbbell above his head. But his arm buckles, and the weight instantly crashes to the ground. "Fuck!"

Behind me, the door flies open. Coop comes walking in.

"Well, well, well," he says, "look who it is." He does a little combo on the punching bag before looking at me for a reaction.

I tell him very nice.

He grins and then turns to Odey. "Fuck Odey. What's the matter, mate? You look like you've done yourself a bit of a mischief."

Odey is still on the ground, writhing around with the dumbbell that's locked his arm to the floor.

"I always lift weights this way," he grunts. "I find it helps me engage my core a bit more. Gives me a better pump." He ends up rolling over onto his front and pushing the dumbbell out of the way, which crashes onto the ground.

Coop turns back to me. "The Pinch is looking for you, Riley."

I wipe the sweat from my face with my towel. "What does he want?"

Coop shrugs, but I can see he is holding something back. I keep looking at him until he looks away.

"The Pinch," Odey rises to his feet and stretches out his lower back, "he doesn't like me, I don't think. He never uses my name. I don't know why."

"Maybe he just doesn't know you." Coop offers.

Odey pauses for a moment. "Perhaps. Yes." A brief silence follows. "But wasn't The Pinch the officer on that job when that fire fighter got burnt a while back? What's his name?" Odey clicks his fingers a few times. "Andrew … Mildew?"

"Merridew," Coop corrects him.

Odey turns his head to the front. "Nah, Merridew's the one who got in trouble for secretly passing union information to the brigade, isn't he?"

Coop shakes his head. "No, that's Mered-ith. He isn't in the job anymore."

"Oh," Odey says. "Right, right."

Coop nods a few times. As if to punctuate this moment, whatever has just been established just now between the two of them, he then says, "Cool," and walks out of the gym, clenching his arse cheeks together

I hear the door shut behind him as he leaves. I turn to Odey, who's still staring after Coop. He screws his face up, thinking something over.

"I'm sure he's got that wrong," he says. A moment passes. "Riley," he says softly, "what did happen that day at that fire last year?"

I turn to him, but I'm quiet.

"I'm just interested. I haven't done anything like that."

I stare back at Odey.

He wipes the sweat across his forehead. "I heard she was really badly burnt across her face and that she got permanent scarring to like seventy-five per cent of her body, so it must have been pretty full-on in there." Odey's getting a bit jumpy because he doesn't know how to respond to me. He grins nervously. "I just think it must have been sort of exciting, I guess. I know it's terrible what happened to that lady, but you saved her, and that's pretty cool. They say she would have died if she was in there any longer, so you know, I just wanted to know about it is all."

I'm quiet. I concentrate on the hum of the aircon for longer than I planned to.

"Oh," his face drops, and he starts nodding. "Oh, OK. Sure Riley, sure."

I lower my gaze and massage my hands.

The moment is broken when the tones sound.

Odey and I shoot each other a grim look. We stare at each other until the electronic voiceover tells us the call is for "Pumper 53A."

Odey groans. "Why us?"

I rise to my feet and make for the door as Odey fumbles with his iPhone by the sound system. "I can't leave it behind, Riley," he yells, "I just don't trust them. They could do anything with it!"

I push through the double doors and head around the couches where the guys are watching something on Nickelodeon

"Busy day for you guys on the A," I hear Frenchy goad. "Send my regards to oblivion."

He then takes a sip from his coffee. But as I walk past, I give the bottom of the mug a little tap.

"Shit," he splutters, "I got coffee on my groin."

I push through the next set of doors to the corridor and slide down the fire pole. I didn't listen to the voiceover, so I don't know what the call is. Still, once I'm in the engine bay, I deviate towards the watch room where Bunker is collecting the printouts of the turnout information.

I pass our truck, where I catch a glimpse of Elvis struggling to pull on his overtrousers – "Oh, come on," he groans – before I make it to the watch room window. Bunker slides it open and hands me the printouts.

"It's a car accident, Riley," he says, "over on Edwards St."

I nod silently, looking at the printouts, and make my way to the truck. Bunker says something to me, but I don't hear it properly. I think it was something about persons trapped in one of the cars, but it also might have just been something about the lunch orders, I can't be sure. Sometimes it's hard to tell the difference.

"There's not much time, Riley," Bunker concludes over my shoulder. I point an index finger to the roof in acknowledgement.

I make it to my side of the truck. I stand in my turnout boots and pull up my overtrousers. There are people watching outside by the engine bay. The doors raise themselves in a deep, mechanical drone, the red warning lights flashing brightly across their faces.

I'm in the truck now. Bailes is in the driver's seat, and Elvis is on the radio, turning us out.

"CXM5, Pumper 53A is out for a reported car accident in Edwards St."

"Roger Pumper 53A."

Odey then appears next to me and slams his door shut as Bailes hits the accelerator. The sirens erupt with a whiny howl, and we tear out of the engine bay, past the onlookers, including a mother and her small child who wave and two girls who beam at me.

We make a hard left onto the tram tracks and then another one onto Vincent St. "Move motherfuckers," Bailes says, as the traffic begins to part in front of us.

I'm still sweating from the gym session, so I don't zip up my tunic (it's a wonder I even put the thing on), and I call out to Bailes, "You know where we're going, don't you?"

He says he does.

We barrel up Vincent St without much hassle, but there's this one car that's sitting in front of us. Every time we change lanes, it merges back in front of us. The car is confused. Then, inexplicably, the driver just stops in the middle of the road.

"What the fuck is this shit?" Elvis throws up his hands. Bailes jerks the wheel, sending Odey flying into me, swerving us around the car.

As we make our way past, I try and get a look at the driver, but the windows are tinted. The car just sits there in the middle of the road and disappears into the background.

I don't know what to expect at this scene. It could be anything. Perhaps just a scratched car sitting on the side of the road with an excited driver saying, "It's his fault, it's his fault!" Or maybe there is no car accident at all, just empty space on the road that we drive straight through, searching for something that isn't there as expressionless faces turn our way and look at us vacantly.

But when we round the corner, I see that today this is not the case. There is shattered glass, a smoking bonnet, which is completely crushed, tire marks on the road leading to another car that has spun itself around on impact. There's someone walking around aimlessly on the road, scuffing his feet with his hands by his sides, and another person sitting in the gutter. His head is bowed, and he is holding one hand close to his chest.

"Right," Elvis says, as we come to a halt, "OK then."

I jump out of the truck and make my way to the nearest car. Someone approaches me from the sidewalk, a woman. She begins hurriedly explaining what happened, that this driver wasn't watching and that he just swerved onto the other side of the road for no reason at all.

She is running out of breath. One hand is across her chest, the other on her forehead, as she tails me to the car. I wave her down a bit and tell her thank you, but just stand aside, please.

She draws in a deep breath, sighs to collect herself, and then shuffles her way off to the side of the road again. "I can't believe it," she keeps saying, over and over.

I make it to the first car. The bonnet is hissing at me, and the windscreen is completely shattered. There is also a trail of blood leading out of the car. I follow it with my eyes to the gutter where the man sits, hunched over himself.

Behind me, I can hear Odey talking to the other driver – the one wandering around the road. "Ah, sir? Hello?...um....how many fingers am I holding up?"

I reach through the window and pull on the park brake to secure the car.

"Riley," Odey calls out, "Riley."

I turn around to see Odey struggling with the wandering driver, who is holding him by the shoulder, collapsing into him. Odey stumbles back a little, but I grab the man by the arm and pull him upright.

He turns his head and stares at me as I stabilise him. I can see some blood trickling down the side of his head. He blinks a few times as his head sways back and forth.

His pupils are dilated, and his eyes are wide. "I know you," he groans softly.

I tell him that I don't think so.

"No," he shakes his head, throwing himself off balance again. "I know you." He brings his head up to look at me a second time. "I never got to tell you the truth."

As he says this, my phone starts buzzing in my pocket. It's not a text message; it's a call. Somewhere, someone's trying to reach me. My name is Riley. I'm the one standing there in the middle with his shirt un-tucked.

I ignore the phone and narrow my eyes for a second as I look into this person. And he just stares back at me with that look on his face, kind of grinning out of the corner of his mouth. I can feel the ringing in my left ear start to rise and then stop.

"Come on," I then say to Odey, "let's get him off the road." We usher him to the sidewalk and make him sit down, which he does with great difficulty.

Elvis is a few metres away from us with the other driver.

He's talking into his radio, getting an ETA on the ambulance arrival. He looks at me and gestures with his head.

I leave Odey with the man (I glance at him as I walk away, but his eyes are glazed back over again – he's not with me anymore) and move towards the other driver.

When I reach him, I ask him where he's hurt, but he doesn't answer. His head's still bowed, and he's all hunched over.

"Buddy," I say, "you OK?"

He sniffs loudly, and then I realise that he is crying. I stand there for a moment, looking at him before he says something.

I don't make it out, but he repeats it a few times, and then I hear it – "I tried my best," he says, "I tried my best." His voice is taut, like he's trying to contain himself. I glance up at Elvis, who's holding onto his radio, staring at the both of us.

"It was never going to work out for me," he wheezes, rocking back and forth.

I stare at him by my feet. My hands are by my sides, and I'm not moving. "OK," is all I end up saying, "OK."

He sniffs a few more times, and he repositions himself a little underneath his arms.

When he looks up at me, I'm a little startled. There's blood all over his face, and he reaches out with his right hand that's torn in half a dozen places. Broken glass is sticking out everywhere, and bits of flesh are protruding from his palm.

He presents his hand to me this way like he's revealing something, a burden he's been holding on to for years that he needs me to acknowledge or understand. He looks me dead in the eye.

I recoil, and he keeps staring at me.

"I'll get the first aid kit," Elvis says and hurries past me.

The man keeps his arm out, but I push it down. I keep one hand on his shoulder and tell him to sit tight. I look back at Elvis, who runs up to us with the first aid kit. He drops it in his haste, and it slides across the ground a bit.

I open it up and stare at it for a while. I don't know what I'm doing - I don't think I've ever dressed a wound on the job before, and I search the kit for answers. Eventually, I go for the saline solution I find on the inside of the lid.

Elvis is looking up the road for the ambulance that's supposed to be on its way. He grits his teeth.

"Hurry up cunts."

I pop the lid and pull gently at the man's sleeve, lifting his arm out into the open. I then spray the solution all over his hand.

I keep an eye on his face when I do this – I'm not sure if this is supposed to hurt or not – but the man doesn't react. He keeps his eyes on the ground, blinking and sniffing.

I hear the sound of incoming sirens, and I know the ambulance is getting near. I look over my shoulder at Odey, who's still kneeling by the other driver. He mouths the words "thank fuck," to me but then stumbles to grab the man as he leans backwards.

The wounds are quite pronounced, and there's still a lot of blood, which seeps back instantly after I spray the cuts with the saline. The small bottle runs out of solution, and I drop it to the ground. I dress his wounds.

The man is still staring at the ground, and I have to tell him to hold the dressings together to manage the bleeding. He nods OK and lightly sits his free hand on the back of the other, pinning his wound between the dressings.

I stand back and look at him. I don't think there's much more I can do.

Some flashing lights catch my eye, and I see the paramedics walking our way. One goes to Odey, the other comes to me. He asks what the situation is, and I just say, "His hand's pretty bad."

The paramedic kneels down next to the man. He then

begins talking to him and taking his pulse before I move away.

The police are on scene and are redirecting traffic around the crash. One of them walks past me.

"Hey Riley, how's the training going?"

I tell him it's going OK.

"Sweet." He keeps moving and yells out to a car, "Slow down dickhead!" before turning around to me and gesturing at the car with his thumb.

I flip my eyebrows and nod.

"Let me know when you're fighting next," he says.

"Will do."

He then continues walking up to the road block where he taps another policeman on the shoulder, who, in turn, glances over his at me.

I feel strange. I don't know why. The phone starts buzzing again in my pocket, but when I check it, there is no sign of a missed call.

I look over my shoulder and see Odey helping the concussed driver into the back of the ambulance with the paramedics. The man struggles to get his foot into the back of the van, but once he does, he turns his head and looks at me. He holds my gaze for a long moment, and it looks like he wants to say something. But Odey pulls him up by the arm, and the man just disappears into the back of the van. I don't see him again, and it's just another unfinished chapter.

The rest of the day overlaps on itself. There's more talk about the union meeting, which I don't go to, and the pressing matters at hand that must be discussed. Spoon puts an announcement over the PA that there are after-work drinks in the city, and Tonto tells me that The Pinch is still looking for me somewhere. There are more calls that we go to, maybe five or six, I can't be sure. Some of them include a suspected overdose by a hobo ("I'm sleeping here, dickheads," he tells us, "can't a guy just get some rest? Jesus!"), a bin fire and a foreign businessman in a lift stuck between floors, who refuses to come out until I yank him through the doors while he's in the midst of a panic attack screaming, "No! It too high! I no do it!"

2.

It hasn't been a bad day, but I'm thrown by something. There's a weird feeling in my chest, and that feeling stays with me when I appear later that night for drinks.

"Riley!" Spoon says, "You made it!"

He shadow punches me and asks how training was. I tell him it was OK. I scan the place. Lefty stands on the edge of a group next to me, grinning and nodding along. He knows I'm there but doesn't want to look at me. Frenchy and Magoo talk about the new recruit we are getting the following week, and Lefty says that he better be able to take a joke because the Fire Brigade is no place for people who can't hack it.

"It's just part of the old school hierarchy," he adds, "and he'll learn his place pretty quickly." There's a sheen of sweat across his forehead, and he keeps nodding his head fervently, up and down.

Everyone has had a bit to drink. The lights from the bar cast a red haze across the sea of heads. Tonto sidles up to me and says something in my ear about how I should ask Stacks about his sister's new boyfriend. "Everyone's doing it, Riley," he slurs.

I point to him.

He grins, points back at me, then taps his temple repeatedly with his index finger. "We all love Stacks, man. He's just great. A real character. We only do it because we love him, right?" His train of thought changes suddenly. He squints as if possessed by some kind of disconnected revelation and disappears back into the crowd.

The music is loud, and the place is packed, which I usually don't like, but I'm comforted by the fact that I'm here on my own.

I see the crowd of familiar faces scattered about, laughing, drinking – I guess I'm here with them, in the sense that they are my workmates, and I am a part of their work life. But I want to leave it there. I don't want them too close to me. And even though the noise agitates me, as does the business, and I can see Miyagi, one of the officers, about to make a drunken scene as he harasses the lady behind the bar, I don't react to any of it.

There's a reassuring catharsis to this. I can stand here by the bar with my beer in the midst of it all, the hum and throb of the music, all the activity, and cut myself off from everything. Something could go down tonight, something bad could happen, and it would be OK. They would only be events for me to respond to. I would be an observer of my own reactions. Because I am not really here. My name is Riley. I'm the one standing there in the middle with his shirt un-tucked.

Someone says, "Riley!" and pats me on the shoulder from behind. I give him a wave.

Odey approaches me through the crowd.

"Hey, man," he says. "Glad you could make it. Rough day man. Rough day." He swigs his beer. "And that car accident was a bit fucked up. I mean, I don't really know. I haven't done it as long as you. But it did seem weird. Did it seem weird to you?"

Yeah, I tell him, it was a bit weird.

"Something about it. I'm not good at putting my finger on things. But it just left me feeling a bit off." He rubs his head with his palm. He says, "My dad had a car accident when I was a kid," and then stops. There is a pause in the conversation, but it's broken when a couple of girls walk up to him at the bar.

"Hey!" Odey greets one of them with a big hug. "Glad you could make it. Riley," he says to me, "this is Em and her sister Joelle."

I say hi.

"Riley's the man. All he does is work out. I mean, does he not look healthy to you? I wish I could find the motivation. Booze seems to be more my thing, though."

I agree.

"Aw, come on." He stands next to me and puffs his chest a bit at the girls.

I tell them, "It's like a mirror, right?"

"Of perfection," Odey adds. He turns to me. "Hey. I met the new guy we're getting next week. He's," Odey pauses, "different, I think. I don't know how to place him. It's confusing." He leans forward to me, like revealing some kind of horrible secret, and whispers, "I don't think he follows footy."

I tell him I don't either.

"But that's completely different." He gestures to me. "Look at you. Apples and oranges." He then glances back at the girls. "But where are my manners? Let me get you some drinks."

Odey orders some cocktails and another beer for him, and we stay there by the bar for a while. After a long silence, Em starts talking to me, and Odey starts to drift into the crowd with Joelle. Just before he disappears, he grins at me and winks. "Oh." He leans in. "I meant to tell you, that guy today at the accident wanted me to tell you something." He says something more, but it's drowned out by the music.

I step in a bit. "What?"

He repeats it, but I still can't hear. I look at his face, trying to read his expression, but it's obscured by people moving around him. His eyes linger on me for what seems a long moment, hidden behind passing faces and outstretched arms handing drinks over people's heads. He looks at me as if something has transpired between us, which unsettles me; I don't know why. And it's this lack of understanding that frustrates me: another reaction I can't pinpoint, something buried, something that wants to come out and present itself to me but perhaps now is not the time.

Slowly, the noise of the bar comes back to me. Odey's face looks away and is swallowed up by the crowd, which returns to its normal speed of activity. I hear Em trying to get my attention next to me, and it takes me a second to snap out of it.

"So, do you like being a firefighter?"

"Yeah," I tell her. I change the topic and ask how she knows Odey.

"I know him through a friend of mine. She was housemates with him for a while."

"Cool," I nod, "cool."

"I never thought he'd end up a firefighter, though. He doesn't really seem the type."

"Well, they don't all look how you think they would." I also add as an inane side note that Odey, of all people, still probably shouldn't be trusted with any kind of heavy machinery. "Or anything that requires the attention above a fifth-grade level."

"You're funny. Do you guys actually save cats in trees?"

I nod and hold up three fingers. "Three cats. That's my number. And a Jack Russell once from a smoky building, but he probably was going to make it out on his own. So that save's debatable."

She nods a few times. "It's not one you can confidently file away in your conscience?"

"No. It hangs about that one. Never really sure how to feel about it."

"That's tough."

"Yeah. But hey, at least I can say I did everything I could."

"And the dog lived?"

"Yes," I say. "From what I know, he prospered. And finally, he chucked it all in and moved to the Bahamas."

"So, what's it like going to fires and stuff?"

I shrug and tell her it gets pretty hot.

"It must be a good feeling saving people's lives. Odey told me this story about you."

I tell her she shouldn't believe Odey; he exaggerates things. I rub at the back of my neck.

She's looking at me with this intrigue, and it makes me uncomfortable. "But you must be so good at dealing with those scary kinds of situations."

"No," is all I say. "Not really."

"Not really?" she repeats.

I shake my head. "It's easy for it to look that way. If there's fire and explosions or blood, it all somehow falls under this umbrella of being brave and heroic from the outside, but it might not really be like that. People make bad decisions or aren't prepared or freeze up, which can cost a lot. Maybe something that looks really brave is actually just wrapped up in mistakes, so, you know, it's not always what it looks like." I say this all rapidly without any breaks. I stop myself when my heart starts beating quickly. But this woman is nice, and she touches my arm gently, which I like.

I tell her I don't like talking about myself. She smiles and says we can talk about other things.

I say thank you, and that's what we do.

The night moves on in a muted sequence. Everyone drinks and laughs and mills about the bar space. I track from Magoo bowing on top of a table to Tonto slurring something in Elvis' ear and then across to Odey, who dances as people clap him on. I see Drillbit leave with a girl who isn't his partner, and Miyagi grabs at a lady who walks by.

At some point, I find myself leaving. Before I go, Em tells me that she likes me. She says that I'm not like the others and that she can see there's a genuine kindness to me, that I'm a gentle man.

But I don't think she knows me well enough to say that.

3.

"No one listens to me, Riley," Stacks says as we push through people at the shopping mall in an endless search for an activated smoke detector that's mysteriously shifting positions on us. I have my tunic open, and my BA is slung over one shoulder. We've been doing this a while now, and the security guard leading us about the place seems lost. A mother points us out to their child in a pram. Another lady takes a photo of us on her phone.

"Sometimes, I just don't know what they want from me. It's like I'm carrying a big sign saying, 'Don't take me seriously.'"

I tell him not to worry, that I don't think it really matters.

"That's easy for you to say. Everyone listens to you. You can say and do whatever you want. It's like I'm under a microscope or something. I say one thing, and people make it out to be something else. Everything is a big joke to them."

We keep moving. Elvis' voice comes through the radio. "Ah, yeah. The panel's actually saying the detector is in Zone 7 now." There is a pause. "Can you guys go there instead?"

"Roger," I say, "Zone 7." I get the security guard's attention and tell him he needs to take us to Zone 7 now. He looks back at me for a long moment, sighs, then gazes around absently before walking off in another direction.

"I wonder what it would take for them to change their minds about me," Stacks says. "You know once I cracked it with Tonto? I mean, really cracked it. I grabbed him by the collar and physically lifted him up and pinned him against a wall."

"Wow," I say, "that's pretty full-on."

"Yeah, I know. And he was properly terrified and everything. But now, if I bring it up with him, he tells me that I'm just a big girl who can't take a joke. That I'm the weak one, for scaring him. There's no winning." He sighs. "They don't do that with you, though. You get to do whatever you want, and no one hassles you for it."

We wind our way around a corner where we walk into a stairwell. I push open the door behind the security guard, and Stacks follows behind me. In my head, I imagine Stacks at my funeral saying:

"Riley made no any effort. He rubbed people up the wrong way, he could screw things up and refused to fit in, but everyone still thought he was cool. Now he's dead; I'm going to be Riley."

I'm following the security guard, who's barely in sight now, winding his way around the staircase. Over my shoulder, I tell Stacks not to worry about it and that I don't really care about that stuff anyway. "People can think whatever they want, mate."

"Yeah," he says, "it's easy for you to say."

But Stacks doesn't know a lot of things. He doesn't know my background or where I've come from. To him, I've just magically appeared this way. Pushed out of my mother's womb as a grown man with nerves of steel.

"It's easy for me, is it?"

"Seems that way."

I pause on a landing. We're at the bottom floor now, underground. I see the door open at the base of the stairs and the shadow of the security guard cast across it. I turn to Stacks and look at him.

"I'm sick of worrying about what everyone is doing," he says. "I'm sick of trying to please everyone." He breathes in. "I guess when I got this job, I thought it would make all of this stuff stop. I'd be a firefighter. I'd be one of the boys, finally. But it hasn't. It's just made it worse." He pauses. "And now I have other problems too." Stacks seems like he wants to say something else, and for a brief moment, he looks at me in this imploring way, like he has something on the tip of his tongue that he needs to tell me.

But the moment passes quickly, and he clears his throat and drops his gaze.

I take a while to respond. "There's a lot of people in this job. And they've all found themselves here for a reason." I'm looking at him, and I know there's more, but I stop myself there.

Stacks deserves better than this, but it's the best I can offer right now. I know what he's going through, and I don't want him to be this way. I want to tell him more, but I just can't. We're here, on this landing, with no one else around, but I still can't talk to him, and it only adds to my frustration because I can never be there when I need to be.

There has been so much dead time in my life lately that I can't get back. I have a lot of delayed feelings that come to me only when it's too late. And then all I can do is try and make peace with it, tell myself that I did the best I could at the time because it wasn't easy for me.

I'm hard on myself. So many things could have been better if I'd done something differently in those moments. I blame myself because it's my fault, and maybe I'll be able to do things differently next time. When I relive those times, I try to give my story a better outcome. I try to keep myself ready because those things might happen again. If I'm lucky, I can rewrite it with a better ending. I can move faster, be better prepared, see everything coming next time around and hopefully be able to let it all go in the end.

That hasn't happened yet, and maybe it never will. Maybe I'll live out my life chasing the ghosts of my past and then just fade away one day when I've become too distant for anyone to notice.

I look at Stacks, and he looks at me. He deserves better, but not everyone gets what they deserve. My mind races, and I start remembering a lot of things.

But all I can do now is squeeze his shoulder for a couple of seconds and move on.

It's later in the day, sometime in the afternoon, and I find myself standing in the rear yard with everyone for a drill The Pinch has organised on one of the trucks. There has been a lot of talk surrounding this. Tonto has theorised that The Pinch is gunning for a promotion, so he wants us all to look busy every time our District Commander takes a break from screwing up our monthly roster and casts his eyes out his office window upstairs.

"It's all about appearances Riley," Tonto whispers to me. "Being in the right place at the right time. Got to play the game."

The other theory floating around is that The Pinch is actually unhappy with everyone and just wants to create pointless work for us. He does this from time to time whenever he feels his authority is being challenged in some hidden way. A couple of months ago, a few of us were late to muster, and we found our monthly drills go up exponentially. However, that particular instance also could have been because Frenchy and Magoo kept misusing the PA system to play Battleship from other sides of the station. No one really got to the bottom of it.

And the other theory is that it's just me The Pinch is unhappy with, and now everyone else is being punished boot camp style.

All of these options seem equally plausible. From what I can see, the drill seems to involve some kind of theory around using the 38mm hose. Still, Miyagi, who's supposed to be running the session, is being continually interrupted by Lefty, who's doing his best to tell us all he knows about firefighting.

There are no breaks in his dialogue. It spills right out of him mercilessly. "There seems to be a lot of debate around when to grab the 38 or the hose reel at a fire," Lefty says. "Do you go for the reel and risk having less water to use and a more cumbersome line to carry? Or do you spend an extra thirty seconds preparing the 38 for action and have better results with the attack but perhaps sacrifice some crucial moments early on? Yesterday, when I was at 67 station, Station Officer McArthur seemed to think the Brigade was making a mistake in discouraging the use of a reel at a house fire, and I'm inclined to agree with him. You see, in my experience, it's all about adaptability, never overcommitting yourself. Sure, the teaching might be this or that. But what you want to do is trust your instinct."

He manages to shift his dialogue a bit. Now, Lefty's coaching us all.

He pushes on. "I would probably do my own size-up of the situation once I hop out of the truck, have a look at the layout of the house, think about how far inside you need to go and other such considerations. If it's fully involved in flame, yes, I would probably go for the 38. You'd need more water and probably wouldn't have to worry about speed so much as the house is beyond saving. It's more just going to be about damage control. Of course, only provided there are no rescues required."

Lefty goes on, and I wonder if he's aware that I know he's only been involved in one proper house fire in the short time he's been in the Brigade, or that there's a big gap between what people think they'll do and what they'll actually do in certain situations, what they want to believe about themselves and confronting the reality behind it. I don't think he's ever had a decent scare before, and it reads plain as day to me in the way he holds himself and the things he says.

There have been a few times I thought I might die. A lot of people outside of my job ask me about this because they're fascinated by it. They want to know what it was like or whether it married up with their idea of a near-death experience. Maybe it was very dramatic, maybe it carried with it some kind of cathartic turning point, a John McClane moment that leaves you feeling empowered or perhaps proud of yourself. You've cheated death and survived because you're strong and wearing a blood-stained white singlet

They also ask if it's true that your life flashes before your eyes. In a way, I guess it does. But with me, it's never really been like that. I've never seen any bright light or drifted above myself through time, calmly watching on as those moments pass by, when I was playing with my first dog or when I made a little treehouse on my own by the beach as a kid. I don't look back on the happy times or have any feelings of nostalgia.

My life flashes haven't been peaceful. Whenever I've had the thought shoot through me that my time is up, all I get to see are the bad things. Because they were all warning signs telling me to watch out. But now it's too late. You're going to die, and it was always going to end this way.

Lefty finally reaches the end of his monologue. He casts his eyes around the group. Everyone is silent.

I say, "Thank you for that, Lefty," and he just nods and stares off into the horizon like some kind of gunslinger.

We're in the truck now, returning from a call to an old lady with a thousand cats who fell over in her flat and couldn't get back up. I tripped on the ladder climbing through the window and managed to sprawl myself out face down on the ground next to her. "Hi," I said, "I'm from the Fire Brigade."

Her front door was deadlocked, and she couldn't remember where the keys were, so we had to break it open for the paramedics to take her away. When we finally put her on the stretcher, she looked me over and squinted. "It's you," she said after a long moment, "Where have you been all this time, my son?" She gently touched the side of my face. "You always were a beautiful boy."

I haven't been sleeping well lately. My thoughts are scattered, and I can't seem to find meaning in anything I do anymore. Sometimes I'm angry, other times I'm sad. But the worst times for me are when I can't feel anything. Sequences play out in front of me, and I just watch on from above somewhere. A muted existence.

I feel that most of my energy goes into appearing normal and covering up who I really am. I can't be this person that lies beneath, so I'll answer your questions, try my best at times to be engaging, and maybe even crack a joke to put you at ease. But it's just a mask. If we all look alike, then no one will panic. But if they knew how I felt when I'm quiet or what I'm really thinking when I look at them a certain way, then they might think twice about how badly they want to hold on to what makes them comfortable.

I'm aware that people like me, that they think I'm strong and that they take to me easily. But none of that matters because they've got it wrong. I feel very differently to them. In fact, the simple truth is I hate myself.

I keep this thought quiet, and it is my own cross to bear. They are wrong to think of me like that, and it is my punishment that I'm reminded of what I'm not every time people give me praise or look up to me in some way. I want this feeling to go away, but I'm not holding out any hope. I want to do it differently next time, and maybe it should be me that gets hurt instead of someone else I'm responsible for. You can sometimes hesitate because you're scared, but so long as you're the one standing up at the end, they will always see it differently.

I didn't need to wait that long before I went in that day. I froze, and no one saw it. I want to change it so badly, but it's done now. It's fair that I don't sleep, that I can't connect with people and that I will not be happy. This is what I deserve. My name is Riley....

Miyagi talks from the front passenger's seat about how he'll stand up for us in this savage union dispute. That we can rely on him to have our backs. He will definitely make sure no Commander tries to stick their nose into our station and upset our perfect workplace because the boys need to be able to be themselves. He looks back at me. I give a nod before shifting my gaze out the window.

Lefty's in the driver's seat, and he's doing his best to agree with everything Miyagi says. They move on to talk about the new guy and how he's fitting in. Lefty says he's already bucketed him twice because it's tradition, and he wants him to feel like he's a valued part of the crew.

We drift down a street somewhere in the city. People with blank faces watch us from the footpath; cars move aimlessly between lanes. The sun begins to set over the horizon in a strangely picturesque way that fills me with an eerie sense of dread.

COTTON NAILS

There has been a bin fire arsonist active in the city recently. He leaves a perfect trail of his movements at night, lighting bin fires on every corner. We've never caught him or even seen him, for that matter. The only evidence of his existence is the calls to his fires we receive anonymously throughout the night. Often, we'll spend half a night chasing him to no avail. Magoo has put up a map in the mess documenting the different trails he leaves. Once he went in a perfect circle around the CBD, but last week the trail made a direct beeline to our station and stopped right out in front. The bin fire was that close; we didn't even need to leave the engine bay. There was no one around either, and I just stood there on my own in front of the flames, putting out a fire that had seemingly started from nothing. I think he works here.

My hands are sore, and I rub them over in my lap. I'll have arthritis in them soon if I keep going the way I am. Odey sits next to me, but he seems distracted. He's quiet, and he stares out the window, not making much effort to talk to Miyagi, who rattles on from the front of the truck. He slowly turns to look at me and holds my gaze for a moment before looking away.

There's a red sky tonight, and it's unusually bright. We pass a park and see families playing, walking their dogs, kicking balls to one another. A father points us out to his young daughter, and she waves at me. I raise a hand as I pass her. And I'm gone as quickly as I appeared.

4.

Time passes, the sun rises and sets, night shifts come and go. I jump the fire poles, I hop in the trucks. At times I get hurt and make big decisions and test myself. At other times I drift along aimlessly. Things happen; things don't happen. And somewhere amongst these overlapping moments, a new day begins.

I find myself walking up the stairs from the car park, passing Brian and Barry from B Shift, who argue with one another about who has the better footy team and whose car would work better off-road in a survival situation. As I push open the door to the station, it's a tangled energy that moves in the opposite direction to the bottom of the stairwell and fades into my background. Stacks believes in ghosts.

I appear through the door in the lounge. CJ is there with Frenchy on the couch. I keep moving, and they ask me how the fight went. I tell them it went OK. I push open the next door to the hallway. I pass another person from B Shift that I don't recognise. He looks at me as I push through into the locker room, where I ditch my bag on the bench and move straight to the mess.

COTTON NAILS

I palm the door open with both hands that remain outstretched for a moment before collapsing to my sides. The remaining firefighters from B Shift are at the table. Everything about this scene is familiar.

As I move past the long table towards my crew, someone makes a comment about the bruises on my face. Coop grins when he sees me. "Here he is," he says. "The big man's in the house." He taps my shoulder as I fix myself a coffee.

He tells me that he came to watch the fight. I tell him thanks.

"That last round," he says, "shit. That was insane."

"Yeah," I say, "I think I just got lucky."

"Didn't look lucky to me." He hits his fist into his palm. "Checkmate."

I finish making my coffee and turn around. Magoo is there in front of me with Tonto and Drillbit. They came to the fight too, they say, and I say cool.

Drillbit asks if he could be the cut man in my corner next time. "I've seen Rocky. I know how it's done."

I smile.

"I saw that tense moment too when the other guy got up in your grills a bit once it was all over. What did you say to him?"

"I didn't say anything to him."

"Yeah, you did. And he backed right off. The ref had to separate you two."

I tell him, no, I don't think so.

Drillbit says, "That's weird. Maybe it just looked that way from where I was sitting." He pauses and says. "But the crowd started cheering a bit when it happened, so something was going on."

I just shrug, no answers.

Drillbit seems lost in thought. He mumbles something under his breath that I can't hear.

Tonto then says that he would have liked to see me take on

everyone if a riot broke out. He says that's what he and the boys would like to see. He adds that there's someone from station 54 that has done some boxing, and I should fight him to prove I'm the tougher guy.

Lefty appears from somewhere and chimes in that yes, he agrees the guy from station 54 is very tough indeed but doesn't go as far as saying anything else that might demand a response from me.

My phone buzzes in my pocket. It's another message from the union. "Urgent," it reads, "everyone check your email. Urgent, urgent."

I put my phone back in my pocket and sip my coffee. Spoon walks into the mess. He slaps me on the shoulder, and I say hi.

Bunker's dry voice then echoes out over the PA system. It starts with a sigh, followed by a flat delivery of, "Attention, attention. Another day has just begun. Endless opportunities await. I want you all to be all you can be, seize the day, embrace the great unknown and report to the engine bay for muster where all your questions will be answered. Thank you."

He clicks off, and we all begin to herd ourselves through the locker room towards the engine bay. Someone says, "Hey Riley, how did the fight go?" I tell him it went OK. Another person whoops behind me and slaps the top of the doorway as we move down the stairs. There's the usual hum of noise, conversations about what people did on their days off, gossip about other firefighters' relationships, speculation about whether The Pinch really is going to get promoted or not, and if he is going to dick us over in the process.

We file through the door to the engine bay. I see Bunker in the watch room on the other side. He looks at me and gives a deadpan salute, which I return. We then begin to line up alongside one another. Odey appears to my right "Hey man," he says, "how you doing?" Drillbit is on my left.

There are a few stragglers, and right before the digital clock on the roof ticks over to eight, Bailes bursts through the door to a dull cheer. He sidesteps, like a footy player warming up, to the far side of the muster line.

Elvis is taking us for muster this morning and goes through the roll call.

"Present."

"Here."

"Sir."

"Correct."

"Available."

"Yo!"

He reaches the end, mutters that we are all here except Stacks, who is sick without evidence today. Tonto adds that "We broke him," and everyone laughs.

Elvis reads out the gear sheet and assigns everyone a truck. I'm on the back of the B with Odey, who taps me on my back when he hears this, with Coop in the driver's seat. Elvis gets to the end of the list and asks us, being a Sunday, if we are going to organise a roast lunch.

Tonto says yes, and expects everyone to join in. "People who split from the lunch will be noted." He scans a warning finger along the muster line.

Elvis nods and says, "Fall out and check the gear." He then turns back for a second, adding that The Pinch is looking for me and wants to talk to me about something.

I nod, and he disappears through the door to the office.

I grab my gear from the cages and throw it on the truck. Spoon puts some music through the megaphone on the Ultra Large. It's 'The Passenger' by Iggy Pop, and it plays in the background as I open the door to the B and pull myself inside.

"Hey Riley," Odey says, already sitting in his seat on the other side.

"Hey, Odey."

He draws in a deep breath, clasps his hands over his face, and exhales loudly. I ask him what's up.

"Don't know, man. Just haven't been feeling myself lately. I think maybe I'm coming down with something. Can you catch chronic fatigue?"

I tell him, no, I don't think so.

"Hmm. Damn. I thought maybe that was it. But it's fine. Up and at 'em, right?"

"Right." I check the radios for battery life, I check the flares are working.

He sighs and sits back in his seat. "Do you ever just feel that we're all just running on a little wheel and going nowhere?"

"Like a hamster's wheel?"

"Yeah."

I look at Odey. He makes a little running gesture with his hands in front of him.

"Tell me about the wheel Odey."

He shrugs. "I dunno, man. No one gets where they want to be, no matter how hard they try. They just stay on the wheel." He gestures again with his hands for a second. "I wish I was stronger and better at dealing with things. But then I think about someone like Tanner – you know him? The guy from 71? He's that buffed up bloke who used to be a jiu-jitsu fighter. Anyway, sometimes I think I want to be a bit like him because no one would mess with me, and maybe shit would be easier."

He pauses, thinks about something for a moment, then pushes on. "But I'm not so sure he's all that anyway. I've seen him get really rattled by things. Just little things too. Stupid things. But no one else sees it because they don't want to. They want him to be this giant badass."

Odey plays with his hands in his lap. "I don't know. I'm not making sense. I guess sometimes I think it's all a bit pointless."

My phone buzzes again in my pocket, but I ignore it. My name is Riley …

"I never move when I need to, Riley. I just stand there like an idiot whenever I need to be brave, and everyone thinks it's funny."

I nod a few times.

"But it doesn't matter. Whatever. I'm just having a bad day." He slaps my arm as he pulls himself upright. "We're going to kill it out there today, man. You and me." Odey gives me a knuckle bump. "The gun crew. Sorting shit out on the streets."

The call comes through the radio like any other job. "Pumper 53B, Firecall." I'm slouched in the back with Odey as we return from a Fire Indicator Panel that activated because some uni student burnt his toast without opening a window.

So, I sit upright, pull a radio from the panel in front of me, fix it to my tunic along with a flare. Odey does the same, and Elvis grabs the receiver. "Pumper 53B, send."

"Pumper 53B, you are out for a reported house fire at 23 Robins St. Fire is in the front of the house and spreading."

"Roger CXM5, Pumper 53B is out for a reported house fire at 23 Robins St."

Coop fires up the sirens and pulls an aggressive U-turn. "Can I get to that address from the Parade?"

I say yeah, you can, and fix my breathing apparatus straps to my shoulders behind me in the seat.

"Pumper 53B, be advised we are receiving multiple calls to this incident."

"Pumper 53B acknowledge."

I look out the window. There's a plume of smoke on the horizon, but I find my attention drifting to the people on the street and the cars pulling over to the side of the road. Someone takes a selfie with the truck as we pass them on a corner. I rest my shoulder up against the window and wait for us to get there.

"The fireground channel is 15 boys," Elvis says.

I echo "15" and switch my radio channel on my tunic.

We make a left; we make a right. We pull up out the front as I hit the release lever on my breathing apparatus and jump out of the truck.

This fire is really going. I can see it's about to make its way into the roof, so we need to be quick if we're going to save the house. I'm on the grass next to Odey, and we don our facemasks together. It's cylinders on, helmets on, grab the hose reel, and move up to make entry.

There's a family crying out the front, and I look at them as we pass by, a mother, a young daughter and a son.

Odey has the hose reel in front of me, and I direct him around the side of the house when I see a window we can safely enter. I have the axe, and I smash it in. I give it a quick ream to get rid of the shards. Black smoke billows out. I then gesture with my head for Odey to make entry, and he does.

"We're in, Elvis," I say into my radio. "Conducting primary search."

"Roger. Just be advised the second crew are still a while off."

It's pitch black in here. I place one hand on Odey's shoulder and give him a tap to get moving. Nothing ever seems to work well in these moments, but we manage to move up the hallway together until we find the fire. Odey opens up the reel from a distance. The steam quickly moves down on us. It's hot, and I don't really know where we are because it's so disorienting. But I stay with Odey and take it one step at a time. Gradually we move up on the fire, bit by bit. I tell him good work, keep it up.

I feel a doorway with my hands, and I yell out for Odey to come this way. I then follow the hose line back a bit and give it a pull, hauling it into the room. Odey is on his knee, and when I feel his shoulder, I push up next to him on the ground.

"Fuck," he muffles through his mask. "Thought you left me."

All we can see is the flame on the roof, and Odey sweeps back and forth with the reel. It's a big house, and it seems even bigger now that we're in darkness. We take a few extra steps into the room. It's really hot, and I realise I didn't put my flash hood on, so I can feel it all around my neck and ears.

Odey pulls at the reel again. "I need more hose," he yells.

"Ok," I tap his shoulder. "Hang on."

He says, "Don't leave me here long, man."

I say don't worry, feel for the hose line and follow it out of the room. I then grab it with both hands and lean right back, heaving as much line as I can. I do this three times. The gear makes it hard to move in, and I can feel sweat running through the inside of my mask. I'm breathing heavily. It's hard work.

I go for another pull on the hose but abruptly feel it yank back in the other direction. I stumble off balance. I then feel another yank. Someone is pulling on the line.

I keep one hand on the line and slowly follow it back. It leads down the hallway towards the window we climbed through. I have one hand out in front of me, and I'm inching my way along the ground with my boot. I can touch both walls on either side of me, so I should be able to feel if someone is on the floor. But when I make it to the window and find nothing, I wonder if maybe there was a door I missed along the way.

I follow the hose line back into the house. I check the hall for doorways but find none. I don't really know what to make of it. When I get back to Odey, I hear through the radio that the other crew is on scene and has made entry on the other side of the house.

"Fuck, where were you, man?" Odey muffles when he feels me next to him. I hit the receiver and notify the other crew that we have possible persons trapped in the house somewhere.

"Roger."

"Did you feel that on the hose?" I yell.

"Yeah, was that you? I fucking fell on my back."

"No. I think someone's in the house."

"What?"

I yell it again next to his ear.

"Shit, if there is, they won't be standing up for long."

"Yeah," I say. "Did you hear anything?"

"What do you mean?"

"Like any yelling?"

"Fuck no. I can't even hear you. Jesus Christ, man, where are we? I'm going to try and move along a bit. Give us some hose, would you?"

I pull again, and we attack the fire on the other side of the room. We start knocking it down, but I can hear it roaring above us in the roof space, so it's not looking good.

I've burnt my neck too, and I rub at it with my glove. Eventually, we come across the other crew. The smoke has cleared a little, and I can just make out the masked figures in the room. One of them looks at me, then looks away and disappears wordlessly back into the haze.

Odey's breathing apparatus starts whistling. He's on low air. I tell him to follow me out the way we came. I keep a hand on the hose line as Odey trails behind. We turn a corner, then another. Before long, I see the light from the smashed window, and we make our way outside.

We head for the grass out the front of the house. There are several other trucks here now. Someone greets us and helps us take off our kit. He hands us a water bottle each and tells us to take a breather.

Odey has his hands on his knees and is bent over, taking deep breaths.

"Fucking hell," he says.

I look back at the fire. The house has become completely engulfed and is now being swallowed up by the flame. Another crew runs around the back of the house with a hose reel. An officer yells something to someone across the street.

The family is still there, and they're all crying. The mother has her hands around both her kids and pats them in a state of shock. I make my way over to Elvis and ask if they're missing a family member inside.

"No," he says. "Good job, though. You guys were on it pretty quickly."

"But there's no one else in there?"

"Not as far as the family is concerned, no. Why?"

I say no reason, and he walks off.

"What's with your neck Riley?" Odey asks behind me.

"I think I burnt it."

"It doesn't really look like a burn."

"What do you mean?"

He squints a bit over my shoulder. "I guess it's a burn. It looks more like a bruise. But it's a really weird shape. Did someone grab you in there?"

I tell him I don't know. We're quiet for a long while. Odey says, "This was my first fire." He then says that he doesn't feel well as we stand there together and watch the house burn itself to the ground.

I'm on my own, having a quiet moment as I change my breathing apparatus cylinder across the street. Someone drops a fresh cylinder next to me, says, "Good fight the other day, Riley," and moves on. I screw on the cylinder. I test it for leaks. I check the low air alarm is working. Firefighters move about the scene aimlessly. The job is over now. The house is rubble, things are quiet, and I'm left with soot on my arms and a strange burn on my neck.

I'm tired too, and my hands are sore. I stay here on my own for a bit and rub my hands over by my waist as I look over the scene. Odey jumps back into the truck, and I can see Elvis and Coop waiting in the front seats. Coop gestures through the window for me to join them – it's time to go. I give a nod and make my way over.

I pass a crew on the street talking about the union dispute. I hear one of them say, "Either you're with us, or you're against us. There's no in-between, and everyone knows it."

I open the door, pull myself inside and tell Coop to drive on. The scene then disappears behind us. We move past all the other trucks, the ambulance, the police officers managing traffic at the end of the street. One points at us and gives a thumbs up. Onlookers become less frequent until they're completely gone, and we're back into a common setting of empty streets with intermittent traffic.

Odey stares out the window. Coop says that he struggled to find a hydrant for us even though there were hydrant indicators everywhere on the street. "It was like a bad joke someone was playing on us."

Elvis' phone then rings. He doesn't really say much except, "OK, OK, right, right." He ends the call, keeps the phone suspended in front of him, turns around and says, "They found Stacks this morning."

"Where did they find him?"

"In his backyard. He was hanging."

Odey doesn't say anything, but Coop asks, "Is he dead?"

"Yes," Elvis says.

"OK." Coop keeps his eyes on the road ahead.

"So. Yeah. He's dead." Elvis waits for a moment. "The guys from 54 found him. A neighbour called it in."

Everyone is silent. Eventually, all I say is that I hope he wasn't left up there for too long. I realise something and check my phone. There's a message sitting there from Stacks this morning. It's a short message. I read it over and nod to myself. I then close the message and place the phone back in my pocket.

It's late afternoon by the time we pull into the station. The gates open slowly for us as we turn into the engine bay and bring ourselves to a halt. Bunker sits in the watch room and stares at us vacantly through the window as we hop out of the trucks. We pull our overtrousers back down around our boots for the next call; we put our helmets back in their carry pouches. Everything is the same.

Elvis says that there's a meeting going on upstairs in the mess about what's just happened. I say no problem and spear off, leaving Odey and Coop behind. I make my way up the stairs, past the Union motto, "Stand fast, stand together". Someone has added to it recently, and now it also reads, "Because brothers don't walk alone in the dark."

I reach the top of the stairs and move through the lockers. When I get to the mess, Tonto is in the midst of addressing the station from the head of the table.

"I know I don't speak for Stacks," he says, "and who could? We don't know how to tell his story."

I take a seat somewhere down the end.

Tonto pushes on. "It's a tragedy," he says, "a damn tragedy. But probably just one of those things that was unavoidable.

And it's really hard to know what someone else is thinking at any point. I guess if he'd made it clear to us that he was having problems, we could have helped, but he didn't. So, what can you do?"

Odey enters the room and takes a seat next to me.

"Now, I don't want anyone here to blame themselves. I saw you all. You all did your best to make him feel like he was one of us, that he was one of the crew. No one can deny that. We treated him no different. Sadly, if I'm being completely honest, I don't think he was really cut out for this kind of work. You have to have a thick skin if you're going to do this job. You have to be able to put up with a lot. And that's why we can be a bit hard with the way we joke around with each other. Because we want to know that the person next to us has got what it takes. If you can't put up with a bit of harmless banter, then what good are you going to be when it comes to the crunch?"

He nods to the room, and others nod too.

"I mean, this is the tricky thing. Everyone is going to be sad about Stacks, and lord knows I am. I'm all broken up about it. But we need to take care of each other. Stacks is gone now, and I'm looking around the room at all of these faces of people who I trust, people who I know I'm going to need to rely on. It's you guys that are the future, and I want you all to know you're in a safe place. This is who we are. We're men."

There are a few murmurs around the room. Frenchy says, "Damn straight."

"We're not here to apologise for who we are. There's a reason why we do the things that we do. And you know what? If we didn't joke around with Stacks do you know what they would have said about us?"

Magoo leans forward. "What would they say?"

"They would say that we were bullying him. It's a proud

firefighter tradition to give someone a hard time. We all do it." He turns to Lefty. "Lefty, when you first came here, all I did was hang shit on you for being a bit of a halfwit. You were always so awkward, and it really sickened me. So instead of ignoring it, I jousted you with it a bit and made you feel like one of us. Didn't I?"

Lefty nods fervently.

"And if I didn't do that, you would have felt left out. You would have felt like we were excluding you. Because we hang shit on everyone – especially the new guys. But now I know you've got what it takes. So well done there."

Tonto scans the room. "I know, men. It's just not fair. We're in a world where people don't understand us. They want to point their fingers and label us with nasty things. It's a snowflake society out there; make no mistake about it. Which is all the more reason why we need to stick together."

People exchange knowing looks. They tap each other on the backs.

"Stacks was a hero in his own way. He's reminded us of the toll this job takes on a man, about how strong we all need to be. And he won't be forgotten. So tonight, we drink to a great man. I propose we dip into the mess fund and throw a little vigil for the memory of Stacks. Beer on."

People are talking now, murmurs of approval. There's a dull cheer going on for Tonto as he raises a finger in the air. A blood-red sky sets itself in the background as he finishes with, "It's what Stacks would have wanted."

5.

It's night shift, and I'm sitting in the driver's seat, staring vacantly ahead as someone crosses the road. He takes a photo of us on his phone before slipping into a group of people on the other side. The group dwindles for a bit and then disappears, collectively, into a doorway off an alley. Some girls look at us out the front of a bar, while some other drunken guy motions for us to beep the horn. I stare at him until he turns back around, mouthing something to his mate, who glances at us over his shoulder.

There's a red light flashing at me, which catches my attention without a reaction, just a look from me that I hold until someone else notices.

"I'm pretty sure that's not supposed to be doing that," Bailes says, squinting over my shoulder as we sit here in the middle of the street, filled with people spilling out from bars and restaurants on just another Friday night. There's a dull hum of activity outside, throbbing music mixed in with laughter and conversation. The red light on the dash continues to flash. "No," he says, "there definitely appears to be a problem."

This is the second time this has happened to us tonight. Two calls earlier, at maybe eleven-thirty, we tried to drive back to the station only to encounter the same problem. And we sat there in the middle of the one-way street until the air pressure built up enough to unlock the brakes and let us drive on.

It's not really a huge problem. Unless we get a fire call through the radio and can't respond. But right now, I just want to get back to the station. The more we sit here, the more likely it's going to turn into one of those nights.

"The air?" Elvis asks from the passenger seat.

I nod.

"Right," he says, "right."

We sit there in silence for a bit.

"Guess we'll just have to wait then."

"Yep," Bailes says. "Guess we'll just have to wait."

I've been really tired lately. I don't know why. But my fatigue tends to creep up on me throughout the day until I can't keep my eyes open anymore. I wake up a lot during the night and get this weird feeling in my lungs that surges and subsides. I also get these headaches from time to time, and tonight, on our last night shift for the week, it all seems to weigh on me a little. And that new one, the ringing in my left ear.

It's been a month since Stacks killed himself, and no one talks about it. "He had problems," they say. Or, "He was one of those ones that never had what it takes." Or, "He was a hero." No one seems quite able to decide.

Earlier tonight, at a call to an activated detector in an apartment building, someone mistook me for his dead son. An older guy in his sixties told me I looked just like him, and I had to say sorry, it's not me, and move on as he watched me from down the hallway. I heard him say something to me before I disappeared but couldn't make out what it was.

Odey sits in the back seat next to Bailes. He's been quieter since Stacks died. He even cried and asked me not to tell anyone, which I haven't.

"Man," Bailes says, "this is bullshit." He glances around. "We're sitting ducks out here. We could totally be set upon at any moment."

"Yeah," Odey sighs. "Mobbed by pissed people."

"Hey man, don't joke; I've seen it happen. Never underestimate the power of booze coupled with the dire need for a selfie. Any second now that door of yours could be thrown open, and a horde of Instagram stars will be all over you, hashtagging the crap out of you without your consent." He gazes out the window. "The panicked face of little Odey sprawled all over the internet."

Odey groans. "Let's just get this truck moving and get back to the station before anything else happens. It's a Friday night, and I don't want to be stuck here any longer than we need to be."

"Patience, Grasshopper," Bailes says.

We fall quiet. Cars have begun tentatively edging their way around us. I glance at the air pressure dial. It still has a little way to go. Elvis asks me how my training is going, and I tell him it's going OK.

"What are you so worried about, Odey?" Bailes asks. "I thought you were keen. Already for action and shit." He flaps his hand against Odey's shoulder a few times.

Odey doesn't really react. "Fuck, you're annoying," he says.

"Oh, come on. Don't be such a sad sack. You're bringing the mood down. Friday night shifts are great. Things happen."

There is something in his voice that bothers me. I'm staring at the low air gauge when it finally flicks over to green. I release the park brake, which thuds into the upright position. "We're back on."

There's a casual cheer from inside the cabin.

Bailes chuckles. "And here's me thinking we were just never going to make it."

We lurch forward, back out onto the road, past the big line out the front of the bar on our left and across the pedestrian crossing, where people scurry out of our way. The street lights resume their familiar sodium flicker overhead. Bailes talks about female firefighters not being tough enough to do what we do. Elvis expresses a similar concern and goes on to say that women aren't funny either.

It's one-thirty, and I'm still hoping for a quiet night. That's what I need. I'm tired.

But I'm still alert, and when a car pulls out in front of us from a side street filled with drunken youths, I manage to hit the brakes with just enough time to avoid a collision. One person hangs out the window with a beer can in his hand and makes this horrible noise, a kind of yell mixed in with a growl, as the car crosses in front of us. For some reason, this plays out to me almost in slow motion, and I take it in before the image disappears up the street to our right, swallowed back up by the night. I'm not sure if anyone else saw this.

"OK, Odey," Bailes says, "so you're in a survival situation. This is a pop quiz, by the way."

"Sure. Go on."

"Your plane has crashed in the wilderness. You've survived with several others. You've recovered some supplies from the wreckage, a bit of food, some cold-weather clothing – not much."

"Ok."

"And there's like a thirty-day trek to the nearest point of civilisation. What do you do?"

"Are there bears?"

Bailes pauses for a moment. "Yes."

"OK. Well, I'd probably craft a few weapons first."

"Good."

"Maybe some spears or something to fend off the bears at night when they test out our perimeter. But also," Odey says, "I'd be eyeing off those survivors suspiciously. Because they're likely to turn on you and take everything you've got. So, keep your spear close."

"Fuck," Bailes scoffs. "That's dark, Odey."

"Yeah, well," he shrugs. "People can let you down sometimes."

There is a pause. "Je-sus. Someone woke up the wrong side of the bed this morning." Bailes then proceeds to make fun of Odey for a bit. Elvis laughs, and Odey ignores it.

We're moving through traffic quite easily now. The flicker of the street lamps has almost become hypnotic, but it sparks some weird memory in me. I lose myself for a moment. My mind wanders, but it shoots back when I hear the radio say, "CXM5, Pumper 53B, Firecall."

Odey groans. "What did I say, man? I told you, didn't I? It's happening. It's now officially one of those nights."

Elvis grabs the receiver. "Pumper 53B, send."

"Pumper 53B, you are out for a reported Emergency Medical Response at 42 Gordon St., The patient, is a 30 to 40-year-old male in cardiac arrest."

"Roger CXM5. Pumper 53B is out for a reported Emergency Medical Response at 42 Gordon St."

Odey groans again. "This is bull-shit!"

I flick the beacons on, then the sirens. I drop a U-turn and barrel our way up through the centre of the road. Bailes tells me to turn left, follow it all the way to the end, then make a right, which should take us to the front door, about eight hundred or so metres up maybe. I tell him, cool, OK. All the guys put on surgical gloves.

I make the turns with enough force to throw us around a little, but I know it's just another call.

We'll get there when we get there.

We pull into the street. Elvis tells me to slow down a little as we scan for the numbers. Bailes tells me it's uneven on his side, so it must be on the other side. Odey reels them off for me.

Sixty-eight.

Fifty-six.

Fifty.

Forty-eight. Forty-six. Forty-four.

"Forty-two." We come to a halt. "That's the one," Elvis says. "I think."

It's a large building, like a warehouse. But there's no entrance we can see. There's also the deep bass of music coming from nearby. I see some scattered silhouettes in the middle of the street up ahead, some more by the building wall. But no one talks to us as we jump out of the truck or tells us where to go. No one is waiting for us.

Bailes grabs the defibrillator, Odey grabs the oxygen kit. Elvis tells us to follow him, and we do.

We move down a path by the building, past a dumpster and a set of bins. The throbbing music is coming from inside the building. We're immediately drawn to it, moving around its edge, past the windows above head height that flicker light and shoot outlines onto the wooden fence next to me.

We take a left, following the edge of the building as it directs us through a strange opening, like a courtyard, before narrowing back down again and funnelling us into a quadrangle, right in the middle of the structure.

But we're yet to come across the front door, and even

though we're surrounded by noise and activity, we still can't find an entrance. We're all alone here.

Elvis asks Odey if he can jump up to the window and try and get someone's attention. He says no worries. Bailes gives him a boost, and he pulls himself up to the nearest window sill.

"Oh man," is all he says. He goes quiet and scans his head around the window. "It's…pretty busy in there."

"Can you wave someone over?"

"I can try," he says. "But I don't think anyone will pay much attention to me."

If there is someone in there who has dropped dead, someone who needs CPR, I know there's a high likelihood that we can't help them. They'll probably not make it out of there alive. Generally, that's the way it goes. I accepted this fact a long time ago, well before this call tonight, well before I ended up standing here with my shoulder resting against the wall, staring at Odey looking through that window, hopelessly waving to people I can't see. So, this prolonged moment of inactivity right now doesn't panic me.

What seems like an eternity goes by, all of us just standing there, squinting up at Odey, Elvis to my right, Bailes cradling Odey's foot between interlocked fingers.

And after a very long time, Odey turns his head, looks at me and says, "Someone's coming."

We find ourselves moving towards a door around the corner. It's not in an obvious position, and after all the turns we've taken, I'm already disoriented. There's a woman hurriedly leading us. It's dark, so I can't really make out her face. "I don't know what's happened exactly," she says over her shoulder as she opens the door. "But you better come quickly."

Immediately we're hit with the full volume of the music. It's quite jarring and washes over us in a way that successfully envelopes us into this other world we've entered. We follow on behind the woman who ducks into the crowd, making her way to the far side of the room. But the place is so densely packed we're not moving very quickly, and it's hard not to notice the looks thrown our way.

I guess it's some kind of electronic dance party. The place is huge. There are couches strewn about, low hanging light bulbs, and empty bottles of beer that bounce off my feet. We pass by a number of booths, each providing a different snap show, one filled with piercing laughter, another with silent heads that follow us, and one more with two people screaming at each other. A bottle smashes somewhere, accompanied by a dull roar.

I'm not really looking around, though. I'm just following. I brush past someone who glares at me while another looks like he's saying something under his breath. The place is pretty dirty, and it looks like the party has been going for a long while but isn't showing any signs of dying out any time soon.

None of us talk to one another, and we keep weaving through the crowd in silence. Odey catches a glimpse of a fight to his right and slows down for a moment, but I place my hand on his back and keep him moving.

Finally, we come out the other side, where the woman leads us to another door. She doesn't break stride and motions for us to follow, which we do.

The door closes behind us, and all of a sudden, it's dark again. "Watch yourselves now," she says, "it's down here."

We're in a staircase. The floor is concrete, and there's a metal railing I'm holding on to as we make our way down. "I had to come up here twice, once more after I called it in, but still, no one would help me. Can you believe that? It's like I was talking into thin fucking air or something."

The volume has died down enough that I can finally hear the distress in her voice. She's tense, but she's holding it together pretty well. "My friends were leaving, but I needed to go to the bathroom first, so I ended up down here where I found him." She sniffs. "But I didn't know what to do, so I tried to call an ambulance, you know? But there was no fucking signal down here. So, I had to run back up to make the call. The lady on the phone tells me that the ambulance is coming and that I need to do CPR. Well, I don't know how to do that. So, I came back down and started banging on his chest. But then I think maybe someone upstairs can help me. So, I run back up and yell out, but fucking no one comes to help. Arseholes."

She sniffs again and leads us down another flight of stairs.

"Shit," Elvis says, "I forgot to book us on scene." He reaches for his radio and hits the receiver but can't get a signal – the radio just beeps back at him.

"We're almost there," she says as we reach the bottom of the stairs. "It's just here."

Elvis pauses for a moment. "The ambos should be here to back us up soon anyway," he says to himself. "I'll do it once they get here."

We make our way down a narrow corridor. "What the fuck is this place?" Bailes finally says.

"I don't know," she says. "But there's a whole complex down here. I got lost and went the other way, looking for the stairs and found more rooms and corridors. It's a rabbit warren."

The place down here is pretty well pitch black. Clearly, it's been used for something in the past, an underground storage facility maybe, I don't know. The music has faded dully into the background, but the pulsing beat still makes its way eerily through the walls. I see the outline of the woman make a left up ahead and duck into a room.

When we enter behind her, there is no moment of horror for us. It's a bad scene – a body of a man lying on the ground not breathing, face contorted and blue – but our movements are numbly procedural. Bailes begins cutting the man's shirt open to attach the defibrillator pads while Odey opens the oxygen kit and prepares the bag valve mask behind his head. It's likely this is from a drug overdose, so no one bothers to make any such comment. Elvis checks his carotid. "No pulse," he says as I kneel down and begin compressions on his chest.

I get to thirty and remove my hands while Odey gives the man two breaths from the bag valve mask. We do this three more times before we have to stop to let Bailes place on the pads, one across the chest on the right side, the other below the chest on the left. Once he's done this, the electronic voice from the defibrillator tells us it's analysing the patient's heart rhythm. Do not touch the patient, it says. We pause momentarily, all crowded around the body. The lady is in front of me on the other side. She asks if she can do anything, but I just shake my head.

We wait for the voice to come back. "Shock advised, stand clear, please."

Bailes says, "Clear all clear," and we hold up our hands to him before he hits the button. The shock is delivered. The voice tells us to continue CPR, and we do.

Elvis tells me he can stand in for me after the next set of compression cycles if I want. I tell him I'm right for now. The rhythm becomes habitual. I count out the last three compressions, and Odey applies the two breaths. We repeat this five times. The machine tells us to pause again. Another shock is advised. Bailes hits the button, and we resume CPR.

It's taken me up until now, after our initial burst of work, to become aware of the warm sensation around my knee. The room is very dark, and the only light we have is a flickering fluorescent on the far wall, so I can't make out what it is. But as I continue with compressions, the light flickers for just long enough for me to see it.

Behind the dead man's head, there is a pool of blood, and it's seeping out onto my knees. This is not a drug overdose. He's been hit with something. Only I keep this realisation private because, at the same time, I also notice someone enter the room.

He stands there in the doorway, staring at us. I can't tell if anyone else has seen him yet or not, but eventually, he asks, "So is he OK?"

I hear Elvis say that we're not sure, but just give us some space, please, the stock standard response we give. I can tell from his voice that he hasn't seen the blood yet, and at a quick glance around, I see that no one else has either. I keep going with compressions at this stage. But I have an eye on the man, standing there in the doorway, not moving.

The lady speaks to him. She was just looking for the bathrooms and found him down here like this, she says. She acted as quickly as she could but couldn't get a signal to call for help. She hopes he is OK, she explains.

But I can't quite work out if they know each other or not. I get Elvis' attention and signal him with a glance. His eyes linger over the blood a long while. I can see him processing this discovery silently. Eventually, Odey and Bailes see it too. They look at me, and I just look back at them in between compressions. They play along and keep up the CPR.

"Right," Elvis says to the man, "um. So, you know him, do you?"

The man pauses. Yeah, he says, yeah, we're friends.

"And I'm just really glad you guys got here. You know. In time."

All the man is to me at this stage is a figure. The flickering light doesn't reach him where he is standing. He is just an outline.

"Well," Elvis says, "he's um. Yeah, in bad shape. We're going to do everything we can, though." I can see him thinking this through. We need to find a way back upstairs to get a signal and call in the police.

Bailes clears his throat. "Actually, Elvis, he seems to be showing improvement. In fact, I think we might be able to handle this on our own." He stares at Elvis. "I think you should go up and call off the ambulance. We don't need them here. Do we?"

"No," Elvis says, "no, we don't. No need to bring them into this."

"Into what?" The man says.

"No, I just meant there's no need for them to come down here when we have it all under control. It would just be a complete waste of their time."

But the man in the door just stays silent. Elvis doesn't move. The silence sits with us for long enough for me to stop compressions and rise to my feet.

The man says, "I think it's best if we all just stay put for a while."

Odey and Bailes are on their feet now too, and we've all formed around each other in a way that makes it clearly evident we outnumber this person.

"Why?" I take half a step towards him, and I notice him brace up just a little. He is still several metres away, and the following events happen very quickly.

Some footsteps begin making their way down the staircase in the background. At the same time, Odey and Bailes move up a little behind me, making the man take a backward step towards the door. The fluorescent light then dies on us completely. He yells out, "In here, now!" And all of us rush him.

Our instinct is to get him out of the door before his crew arrives. But because it's pitch black now, we end up slamming him straight back against the wall behind instead. I have my forearm against his chin with my full weight behind me, locking his head to one side. But he's a big guy, and we struggle to hold him. He's screaming out now, hurry, hurry, and I can feel everyone else around me, grabbing at him and flailing in the darkness.

It's absolute chaos. There is screaming coming from everywhere, and I can't make out who is who. Collectively, we manage to shift him towards the outline of the door to the right. I then drop my shoulder and force him through the empty space, just as the other figures arrive behind him.

Someone – Elvis maybe – grabs the door and slams it shut on him, only the guy has managed to pry his arm in between. As we all pile up against the door, we crunch his forearm, which flaps about next to me.

It's now our weight against theirs, and we dig in the best we can. Odey is right next to me and has his back flush against the door. I can see his legs outstretched as he pushes with both feet. I've still got my shoulder up against the door, and I can sense the man's face just around the other side. He screams in pain while he hits at me with his jammed arm.

Someone starts ramming at the door on the other side. At first, it doesn't have much effect, but I hear them yelling to one another. Before long, the others start joining in. They begin to get their timing right, and the door starts pushing us back.

We're panicked. Bailes yells, "Fucking push. Jesus," but the guy's arm is still in the way. Someone appears around me to my right. It's the woman. She grabs the arm and pushes it up above her head. I keep my shoulder against the door, digging in with my feet as I help her push it with my right hand.

"Just a little more," she winces into my ear. She then pulls at something above my head, and I hear something hit the ground. His arm is right on the edge of the door now. We then wait for the next ram from the other side to push his arm out completely.

I grab at the handle as she goes for the lock. I wait to hear it click into place before I let myself slide down the door onto the ground. The door handle above me jiggles a few times. I hear them talking to one another in muffled tones on the other side.

Odey is next to me on the ground.

"Fucking hell," he wheezes, in between breaths, "fucking hell. They killed that guy. They fucking killed him. Jesus."

I'm trying to catch my breath too, and everyone just sort of sits there in silence as we process what's happened. The woman's voice is the first to break the moment. "Is everyone alright?" she says.

No one answers. So, I say, yeah, we're good, I think.

Her feet appear in front of me. I see her reach down for something on the ground. It's a knife. She picks it up and holds it by her side as she stares at me. "You're bleeding," she eventually says.

I look down at my shoulder and realise it's covered with blood. "Yeah," I say, "he must have got me."

"Holy shit," Odey is saying, "what the hell just happened? What did we just do? They were trying to fucking kill us. Am I the only one fucking terrified here?"

But we're all scared. And we need to get ourselves together quickly to work out how we're going to handle this. I can hear murmurs on the other side of the door. They're beginning to get organised. Odey repeats, "What the hell just happened?"

"We've seen something we shouldn't, Odey," I stand up. My shoulder is throbbing, but I don't feel any pain yet. "The guy lying over there didn't OD. He's been killed. Right? And there's a lot more of them out there now. So, we really need to keep our heads here. OK?"

"Well, why the fuck did they kill him?"

"Who cares. He's dead. And we're stuck in here until we work something out."

Bailes is being really quiet. I can see him with his head in his hands on the ground as Elvis paces up and down next to me. "OK," he says, "OK. We don't have a signal down here, so the radio is no good." He stops for a moment. "But the ambos are still coming. Yeah. They're still coming, and they should be here any minute." He's whispering this to me, right up close. "All they need to do is get anywhere near us, and we can yell out to them."

"Yeah," Bailes stands up. "All we've got to do is keep that door shut until then. They'll hear us in here and call in the cops."

I tell them it's probably no good. "We haven't booked on scene, so no one even knows we're here. They'll probably just wave on the ambos when they get here, too. There's a lot of people up there, and we don't know how many more of them are friends with these guys. If not all of them."

"Fuck," Bailes whispers, "fuck, fuck, fuck."

But we're interrupted by a voice through the door. "Hey there," it says. Odey jumps up to his feet next to us, away from the door. It's a new voice, a different person. "We're really sorry about what just happened. I know it must have given you a scare."

None of us move, and we all just stare at the door.

"But I think it's just one big misunderstanding. You see, our friend has been hurt. And we just want to make sure he's OK." There's a pause. "Is he OK?"

I'm not sure what they're trying to play here. So, I make my response noncommittal and just tell him, "He's in bad shape."

"Well," the voice says. "I know you're probably all a little worried. So, I'm not going to suggest that you let us come in there. But maybe you could place him by the door, and we could pull him through to our side."

No one says anything to this.

"We just want him with us," the voice adds. "You'll only need to open the door a little bit. We don't even need to be there if you don't want. You can just push him through on your own."

I just stare back at the door. I then hear some more whispers on the other side.

"We'll give you a minute to think it over, I guess."

There are some dull footsteps. It sounds like they're moving away, but I can't be sure. I then hear someone re-approach.

"Hey. Are you there, tough guy?"

It's the other voice now, the first guy, and he's talking to me. "You've done a nice number on my arm here. But you just got me when I wasn't ready. Maybe later you can try and charge me again. I'm curious to know how you'd handle that without your friends to help." There's a short pause before his voice trails off. I then hear him tell me that he owes me one, and his footsteps disappear.

"What the fuck is this?" Bailes says. "They know he's dead. They're the ones who did this."

"We're not opening that door," I hear Odey's voice somewhere. It's taught like his neck has been wrung. "No fucking way. They're fucking crazy."

I turn to the woman and ask if she knows these guys. What's her connection here? What are we in for?

But she tells me she doesn't really know. "I just came here with friends. And they're gone now too."

"You think they'll come back for you?"

"They'll just think I bailed on them. So probably not." Her voice is much more level now. She asks me how my shoulder is, and I tell her it's still pretty numb.

"It doesn't make sense," Bailes says. "They know we're not dumb enough to believe them. They've clearly done this. Something else is going on."

Odey is hyperventilating. "We can't let them in," he says, over and over. "We can't let them in. We can't let them in."

Elvis gets down in front of him. "Easy," he tells him, "easy. Breathe, mate. Breathe." He's doing his best to soothe him, but I can see he's on the brink himself, too. He tells Odey that it's all going to be fine, that we're going to work this out and reason with them and that it's all been one big misunderstanding. He says this last bit twice; I think more for himself. But it seems to work, and Odey starts calming down.

"It'll be OK, mate," Elvis says, "we'll be fine. Won't we, Riley?"

"Yeah," I say, watching on from a distance.

Odey rubs at his eyes and sniffs. "I'm OK now," he says, "I'm OK. Don't mind me. I've just haven't been myself lately, I think, is all this is. That's all this is. It's just a bit much for me right now. But I'm fine. I'm going to help out. Don't worry. I can do this."

He goes to talk about something else but stops himself. I hear him take a deep breath. "Guess it's really turned into one of those nights, hey?" He tries to laugh.

But I just nod a little, staring back at his outline on the ground, hugging his knees to his chest. My mind wanders, and I feel something in me surge momentarily. It rises, then subsides.

My trance is broken by some noise behind me. "They must want something he's got on him," Bailes says. He's searching the body. "There's no other reason." His movements are hurried, and I can see him pulling at pockets and pushing the body around. "There must be something."

As he's doing this, the woman starts making her way around the edge of the room. It looks like she's grabbing at all the furniture, shelving and other trash that's scattered around and begins pushing it out from the walls. She mumbles something under her breath. It sounds like, "I'm not going to die tonight."

"OK," Bailes says, "This guy's got a set of keys, a wallet and a phone." He takes a breath - he's talking very quickly. "Now, I think it's the phone they want. This guy's already dead. Someone's clearly killed him. Probably that guy who first walked in."

As he's saying this to me, I bend down and touch the back of the dead man's head. I feel shattered bone on my fingertips. A bat has done this, maybe. Or any kind of blunt object.

"So, they're not trying to save him or anything. But they want something." Bailes looks into his hands at the items. He goes to talk but then holds up a finger to me. He needs a moment.

I take the items from him, and he sits down.

I know we don't have long. They will be back soon, so at this stage, we just need to buy some time. I glance around at the scene. Elvis is still talking with Odey, Bailes is next to me on the ground, the woman is behind me rummaging about doing something, and I'm standing here in the middle of the darkness with a dead man at my feet. My shoulder begins to throb a bit harder.

When the voice comes back through the door, it doesn't make me jump. "Hi," it says, "so here's what I think we're going to do." I notice the direction of the voice changes as he speaks – he's looking around at something out there when he talks to us. "I'm going to back right off. All the way up the hallway. I'll talk to you from there, so you know where I am. And there's a small gap under the door, so you can check no one else is standing around. Then, when you're comfortable, you can open the door, push out our friend and close it straight back up again. So, everyone will be happy."

There's a short pause, during which I hear him ever so quietly push at the door a few times, testing its integrity. There are a few whispers too.

"So, what do you say?"

I glance at the items in my hands. My response comes out very quickly. "Maybe you just want his phone?"

There's a pause followed by a few more muffled whispers. I keep my eyes on the door. The silence is enough to answer my question, and my heart rate jumps up.

"So, you can get the fuck away from the door. And your mates. Or I'll put my boot through this phone and destroy whatever you're after."

I don't know if this will work. I have no idea what it is they want on the phone or if there is some other way they can access it. But the voice says, "Sure. OK. Take it easy," and I see the dim shadows of feet move away from the bottom of the door.

I tell him to stay the fuck away from us, and if I hear anyone walk within five metres of that door, I'll be kicking the shards of the shattered phone under the door for him to sort through.

"Alright, champ," the voice says from a distance, "have it your way." A set of feet make their way up the stairs quickly. Someone else whispers something in the background. "Just don't go doing anything silly. I don't want this to get any worse for any of us."

OK. It's worked, for now. I glance around absently, then look at the phone. It's password-protected, so I can't access it. It goes in my pocket, and I check my watch again. I then pat my hands around on my other pockets. I have nothing to use as a weapon.

"Nice work," Bailes says.

I tell him it's probably only going to hold them for a little bit. "They'll be working out a way to breach this place real quick before we can work out what's going on. We can't be here much longer like this. We're going to have to work something out."

"Fuck man," Bailes lowers his voice. "I don't know if I'm ready for this shit." He giggles and then stops.

"I've found a duct," the woman says behind me.

I turn around. She's pulled everything into the centre of the room.

"It was behind the cabinet there."

"How big is it?"

"Big enough. Maybe."

"Do you still have that knife?"

"It's not leaving me." She waves it next to her head.

I nod, OK.

We're starting to think now. The mood is changing, although my hand still shakes, which happens from time to time. But tonight, there is no need to hide it in my pocket, like I normally do when my mind wanders, and the headaches squeeze at my temples. It's dark. No one can see me now. And what normally frightens me doesn't anymore.

Despite the horror of this moment, the random nature of it, there's a part of me that's not surprised, that somehow expected it. Of course, this would happen. I've seen this coming for a while now, since that time four years ago in a fire when a wall blew out in front of me, missing me by inches. Or when I held that lady by the hand after her car flipped on her and told her that it would all be OK as she cried and died. It's been creeping up on me bit by bit, and I should have known better.

I don't like that that it's made me this way. I can't relax

anymore, and I don't feel things the way that I used to. I know it's going to be bad tonight, and it makes me sad because I don't want to be this person anymore.

Bailes asks if I have any ideas. I tell him I noticed another stairwell exit on our way in. "Maybe we can get to it from somewhere down here."

"Well, that sounds good to me."

I stare back at him in the darkness. I ask him how he's feeling.

"Tiptop," he says.

I nod. I don't know how we're going to hold up together, but we need to move, and we need to do it quickly. There's no grand master plan. We just need to get out of this room. It might go our way; it might not.

But I've never really been good at sitting still anyway.

6.

"Ok," I position myself under the duct, "are you ready?"

"I don't know," she says. "I haven't really done this sort of thing before." She stops just in front of me. She's tall, I realise, about my height.

"Just make sure you stay quiet. And when you get to the other side, whatever is there, try and stay hidden. Get away from doors or open spaces if you can," I say. "We'll be right behind you."

She looks back at me for a moment before she tells me that her name is Dom.

"Riley."

"Well, it's nice to meet you." Her hand sits on my shoulder for a brief second before I give her a boost, and she disappears into the duct above me.

Bailes is next. He doesn't say anything. Just gives my shoulder a squeeze and vaults himself out of sight.

Then Odey. "I know I'm not much good at this," he tells me, "but I'm going to really try this time." And finally, Elvis.

I look back towards the door. I can't hear anything, which makes me nervous. But I've passed the point of indecision. I take a morbid comfort in knowing that this is our only option. The dead man's phone still sits in my pocket, and I give him one last look, lying there on the ground in a pool of blood that has expanded to where my feet now stand. We're leaving him here, and even though he was already dead on our arrival and there was probably no chance of us ever saving him, I know this will register in some way. Later this will bother me.

Part of me hates him for bringing me to this place, for putting me in this situation only to experience another failure and uglier realisations. But he's made some decisions himself – bad ones – and that's why he's here too.

They always say you did the best you could, but it's never true. You look for the holes and focus on them until they become the only thing.

I don't know what will happen to his body or who out there will worry about him now that he's gone. There is no one here to hug him in his moment of death or ask us if there is anything else we could do. He's just a lonely, nameless outline, lying there on the ground.

But I have an opportunity here to make things right. This time things will be different. I'm ready, and if I make it out of here, I'm not going to walk away feeling guilty. All of that needs to stop. I need to let go of those moments tonight, all of them. They are from the past, and they won't hurt me anymore. But it's going to get worse before it gets better. And even though my problems won't stop, maybe I'll at least be able to feel some relief. Maybe I can be kind to myself again. I don't know if it works that way, but I guess I'll be finding out soon enough.

This is what I have been waiting for all this time, and now I get to confront it in this dark underground complex where no one can find us.

I was meant to end up here tonight.

COTTON NAILS

    I feel my mind wandering but snap out of it as I hear some quiet thumping from above. I see Elvis stick his hand back out of the duct for me. It sits there for a moment before he wiggles his fingers about.

    So, I take a leap, grab his hand, and pull myself in.

7.

I'm pushing myself along the dark tunnel now with my face pressed down on the floor and my hands locked in front of my chest. The duct has a high ceiling, but it's tight and hugs my shoulders in a way that constricts my breathing. I can hear the hum of music upstairs. I can hear Elvis pushing himself along in front of me. But I can't hear anyone else, and I know there is a very real possibility they have already run into trouble on the other side. I don't expect our situation here to end well.

But I want to try. I don't want to push away the little hope I have just yet.

I keep pushing myself along the duct, which winds itself around several corners. It's hot in here. I'm sweating, and the deep cuts on my shoulder sting against the wall, but the adrenaline keeps most of the pain away.

I feel Elvis' weight drop in front of me. He's out of the duct. I know I must not be far off. I still can't hear any voices, so I'm careful when I exit on the other side. I drop down to the floor quietly and stay on my knees for a moment as I look around.

The silence bothers me initially – oddly, it reminds me of

something else, another time, I think – but when my eyes begin to adjust to the room, making out the profiles of the four other figures positioned there, my readiness holsters itself for the time being. There are a few tables I can see, and they're connected in a square in the middle of the room, separating me from Elvis on the other side.

Dom appears behind me and asks, "What is it?"

I tell her that it's a clan lab, I think. It looks like there are beakers and bottles strewn about, lots of containers with liquids in them. I don't touch anything, and it quickly dawns on me that we need to keep moving.

Bailes says he is going to make a weapon from a bit of glass he's found on the ground. He says that we should all make weapons.

I tell him to keep his voice down.

He reaches down, and I hear him pick up the shard of glass. "I always wondered how I'd handle a situation like this." He pauses. "I think we're all better off getting ready." He wraps what looks like a bit of cloth he's found around the base of the glass as a handle. "Come on," he says, "we'll all have something to fight back with."

Elvis tells him to be quiet. "We don't have time for this. They've probably already worked out we're gone," he whispers, but Bailes starts rummaging around on the ground.

"Yeah," he says, "exactly." He's making more noise now, though, and it's making us nervous. I grab at his arm, but he yanks it away.

There's a doorway behind me, I notice. It's open, and I stick my head through to find another hallway.

"Don't want to be caught again unprepared," he says, then adds, "don't make me argue."

"Bailes," I whisper, "stop moving," I tell him to calm down, but he won't. He's making a decision now for all of us. I quickly ask Dom if she's ready to move, and she says she is.

"Please, man," Odey begs, "please. They're going to hear us."

"We don't have much time," Bailes says. "Help me with these beakers. We can use the connecting rods as weapons."

Elvis holds out his hands in front of him. He's trying to talk him down a bit, but it's useless. Bailes is losing it, and no one can stop it. All I can do is just watch on with a muted acceptance.

It's like I've already made up my mind, like I'm already miles away, somewhere else, and the moment means nothing to me because the outcome – a bad one – has already determined itself. I'm not here. I'm not present. There is a sequence of events that I've preempted right now, and my brain processes it so quickly that it plays out before me in a way that makes me move on before it even happens. Because I know that it was simply always going to be this way. It has been decided. It's done.

This sort of thing happens to me a lot, a kind of nightmarish horror show in my mind, a rapid-fire sequence of images that warn me of what could follow. Sometimes I'm at peace with the images, and they sit there quietly like wordless ghosts in the background. I'm wary but not alarmed. Other times they scream at me. My skin crawls, the heart pounds, but I'm ready.

So, keep your back to the wall and get ready to move. Don't hesitate, switch gears, and know that you can do anything you need to.

I see them emerge behind Elvis, maybe half a dozen dark figures that envelop him so quickly he only has time to silently look our way one last time before they're on him. "Please no. No, no, no, no," he's gasping.

They're stabbing him. I can hear the thudding of the blades making their way in and out of his body.

Bailes is next. He swings his shard around. It looks like maybe he connects it with someone once before he is face down on the ground, amidst several arms pumping in and out on top of him. He makes a few groans, and then he stops.

This happens within a period of seconds. We're all the way on the other side of the room behind the tables and clan lab. There's nothing we can do.

I'm already palming Odey and Dom behind me and backing out the door. I catch one last look at the scene, a snapshot for a future memory, processed and dismissed in the time it takes me to slam the door behind us.

We then begin the last run for the surface.

We're crashing along the hallway now, the three of us rounding corners and beating on locked doors. There's no plan left, and we're reduced to a blind charge. I've become completely reactive now. I have no more concerns or inhibition. Everything that I normally work too hard to push down has bubbled to the surface. This is who I really am, and you will see this around my eyes if you look long enough.

The throbbing music from upstairs is getting louder, and I know we're close. We round one corner, we round another. I eventually hear Odey yell out, "This door, this door," and I make my way to him. It's hard to differentiate between our voices and those faceless figures screaming to one another on our tail. But in the midst of the noise, I think I hear Dom yell for me to hurry.

When I enter through the stairwell door, Odey is being worked over with what looks like a bat. He's sunk to his knees in the corner as the guy lays into him with big, overhand strikes. Dom has been knocked to the ground next to him. I glance at her briefly before I move up on the man and give him a right hand to the head that sends him down. I then take another step and give him several more as he lays there on the ground.

I've become mechanical with my movements. There's no emotion to it. I grab the man by the collar and lift him up off the ground. His head hangs limp, so I know I have a few moments to get organised.

I end up rolling him on his side and kneeling on his head. Dom's feet appear again in my field of vision. The knife is by her side, and this time she extends it to me. I take it from her and move it to his throat.

It takes me only a few seconds to weigh it up. Odey is badly wounded and probably can't walk. The voices are getting closer, and the man under my knee is regaining consciousness and beginning to thrash about.

It takes me only a few seconds, but I make the decision, and his throat gets cut. It's an aggressive move, but I do it quickly. He gurgles and thrashes, and as soon as I'm done, I'm up next to Odey, pulling him to his feet. Dom tips a cabinet across the door, which is immediately pounded on the other side. "I still owe you, one tough guy," I hear screamed through the gap.

Odey is wheezing. He's in a lot of pain. I tell him it's going to hurt, but we just need to move. I put his arm over my shoulder, and he screams. Before I know it, Dom is on the other side of him doing the same, and we're making our way up the stairs.

We're pretty much dragging Odey along, one step at a time. It's not easy. But after the first flight of stairs, I can see the light where the door is. No one is talking. We're just fixated on that door.

When we get there, there is no hesitation. I kick the release latch, the door flies open, and all of a sudden, we're back amongst the party. Everyone is looking at us. We have absolutely no idea what to expect, which of these people are involved or know about what has just taken place downstairs in that darkened area.

In the light, I notice that we're all covered in blood, and the crowd just silently parts for us as we make our way for the exit. The music volume seems to have increased, and I can barely hear Dom when she says, "This way, this way." She pulls to the left, and I redirect myself. The dead man's phone begins buzzing in my pocket.

No one says anything to us. No one helps or intervenes; they all just stare at us. It's a sea of turning heads, following us as we move across the floor.

When we make it to the door, there is an eruption of noise behind us. At a glance, I can see movement coming our way through the crowd. But there are not many options now, so we just keep going.

We push through the door as Odey's legs give way. We pull him back up and make our way out onto the street. It's a different way to how we came in. There's no fire truck in sight, but we instinctively move towards the busy end, near the bars up the road.

There are people around now, people coming home after a night out to see the three of us, bloodied, dragging ourselves down the middle of the street. We're still oddly silent – neither Odey nor Dom cries for help – and this reality must be as strange for them as it is for us.

Everything is quiet. Apart from the odd murmur from onlookers, our footsteps and breathing are all I can really hear. It's cold out here, and our breath vaporises in front of us. We don't slow down.

I then make eye contact with someone on the footpath.

He looks at me, shuffling along with Odey's arm across my shoulder as he stands there after a night of boozing, only to be confronted with this image. The way I look back at him - it's a look that says, 'what are you standing there being so shocked at?'

He holds my gaze, doesn't budge (there is a phone in his hand that he doesn't use to call the police), and a brief moment of wonder shoots through me about what story he will tell himself when he goes home. I want to know how he processes his inaction, trivial as it is, in this particular moment, whether he will change any expectations he has or go the other way and bury them in a nicer narrative that is simply untrue. He's just watching, comfortably doing nothing, not taking any stance.

It's a look that spans a few long seconds. Eventually, I turn my head, and he disappears behind us into insignificance.

A few more moments pass before I hear the footsteps in pursuit. I wait until they close right in on us when I finally bring us to a standstill. I turn us all around, Odey slumped in between Dom and me, our chests heaving for breath.

It's just him on his own. He has a bandage around his arm where we slammed it with the door earlier, and he comes to a halt in the middle of the street in front of us. We stand there looking at one another for a long moment. I don't move, and neither does he.

He studies all of us under the street light. We've stopped running, and there is a feeling in the air that it's over, that he is now just imposing on a scene to which he is no longer welcome. He is an interloper in his own story.

It's all changed, and I can see this confuses him. Somewhere in the distance, the sound of approaching sirens push their way through the night. Slowly he drops his gaze. He takes his time turning around and then simply just plods his way back down the street. We watch him until his figure blends back into the shadows.

He's gone, and we stand there for a while until this realisation washes over us completely. "I'd like to sit down now," Odey says.

I tell him sure, and we carefully lower him to the ground. He winces, hangs his head and rests his elbows on his knees. I ask if he is OK for the time being, and he just nods.

"So, I guess he's not coming back then," Dom says.

"No," I say, "I guess not." I turn to her. It's the first time I've actually seen her properly in the light. She smiles weakly at me.

The dead man's phone then starts buzzing again in my pocket. Hesitantly, I reach for it. It's from a private number, and I hold it in my hand as it rings away.

"Do you want to answer it?" Dom asks.

I think about it for a while before I tell her no. "It doesn't matter anymore." I leave the phone there on my hand for Dom, but she just stares at it until it rings out. The screen says, 'You have 23 missed calls'. I do a double-take at the phone when I think I see a message from the Union. I then put it down on the ground. The sirens get a bit louder.

"Hey Riley," Odey says on the ground, "I just realised we start our days off in a few hours." He pauses. "Guess we might get some overtime tonight, though." He starts shivering uncontrollably.

I sit down and push up next to him. Dom does the same on the other side, and we sit there, the three of us in the middle of the street. People gradually inch their way closer to us.

"It really hurts now," is all he says.

I tell him I know. We can see the flashing lights reflecting off the building walls down the street as they close in. Someone films us at a distance on their phone.

"It's been a rough week," Odey says in between breaths. "Maybe I'll go out tomorrow. Tonight, I mean. It's my friend's birthday, but I might need to rest. I also need to clean my apartment." He then says that he thinks his ankle could be broken.

There's a police car in the street now. It's coming towards us. The lights are still going, but they've cut the sirens.

Dom asks if I got a good look at that guy just now. I tell her not really.

"Me neither," she says. "Oh well."

The police car comes to a halt in front of us. The doors open, and two figures emerge. I know this is the end of one thing and the beginning of another. It's another chapter to be filed away.

The two of them approach. Their uniforms are clean. I can smell fresh coffee from their car. They stop and look us over for a moment. The one on the left then says, "You really shouldn't be sitting there in the middle of the street like that."

My name is Riley. I'm the one standing there in the middle with his shirt un-tucked.

COTTON NAILS

Shawline Publishing Group Pty Ltd

www.shawlinepublishing.com.au